GRADY A. SIMPSON

Crossroads and Redemptions: Stories for Life's Winding Paths

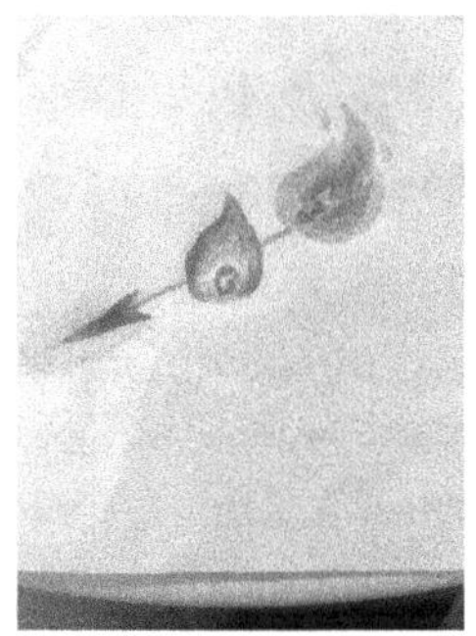

First published by Brother Gas Books.Com/Publishing 2026

Printed in the United States of America.

LCCN 2026906850

First edition

ISBN: 979-8-9948208-0-3

Editing by Peter Lundell
Editing by Robin Reed
Advisor: Seralynn Lewis
Cover art by Barry Hansen
Illustration by Abigail Tolor

This book was professionally typeset on Reedsy.
Find out more at reedsy.com

Contents

Acknowledgments

My sincere thanks to the following people and organizations:

Peter Lundell, developmental editor, a man of faith, patience, and friendship.

Seralynn Lewis, author, friend, and Christian guide.

Abigail Toler, Illustrator

All my friends in the Charlotte Chapter of the American Christian Fiction Writers, who

patiently endured all my questions.

My family, for all the support, encouragement, and love that kept me going through the

book-writing process.

1

Chapter 1

"THE WHIRLWIND"

David Manker's conscience didn't bother him about skipping church today. He deserved a Sunday off. After 10 years of the same old religious routine, he felt drained. He needed to relax and go fishing. What could be better than spending a whole day fishing?

Nothing can ruin this day, right? "Nah, it ain't going to happen."

If Deacon David caught enough tasty Sunday trout, he'd invite the preacher to dinner. A slow grin spread across his face. David chuckled at the thought of watching the preacher eat the Sunday-caught fish.

Every Sunday, the church service followed the same routine and bored him. But today, the church gossip would find something new to discuss. Deacon David Manker wouldn't be there to shout "amen" during the preacher's sermon. After ten years, the amen cadence became a habit and was no longer useful.

Unfortunately, Deacon David hadn't yet realized that what he thought was boring was actually a gift of life, and that life is fleeting. Vapor can dissipate quickly. He ran a hand through his graying hair, a familiar nervous habit.

David's loving wife said he felt sick and regretted missing church. She also did everything she could to support her husband by shouting "amen" several times during the service. He pictured her strained smile, a smile everyone could see from the back pew.

The old church bells tolled, and their sound drifted through the air. As he adjusted his fly-fishing lure, David frowned at the bells. Today, he chose fishing over church. Besides, God made fish for people to catch and eat.

As he cast his line, his fishing boat, The Holy Cross, rocked gently, and the fly lure dropped onto the clear, still waters of Trent Creek. He hoped the trout would bite his beautiful lure. He leaned back against the cool metal of the boat, closing his eyes for a moment.

David relaxed into a nap, seeing people heading to church. First, Deacon Eddie opened the church doors and rang the bells. Then, Flora Mae entered through the church door and praised Deacon Eddie's punctuality and dedication. After that, she hurried off to her Sunday school room to prepare their lesson. Finally, the pastor entered through the back door after finishing his morning prayers.

***

Something tugged on the fishing line. His gaze darted to the rod tip, and his heart pounded. He jerked upright to resist the tug and drive the fishhook deep into the fish's jaw. But to his surprise, something had taken the fish—or lure. Instead, bubbles rose to the surface, circling, and the fly reel whined as it rapidly let out line.

The swirl shaped itself into a widening hole. Had a fish pulled the lure down that far and that fast? A faint mist rose from the swirling vortex, and David laughed out loud, assuming the wind had whipped a dust devil over the water.

He slapped his knee with an easy grin. He had never seen anything like this. Could it be a waterspout instead? He needed to start his engine to escape from the growing waterspout, but he didn't want to let go of the fishing rod. His fingers ached as he held the cork handle tighter.

The mist thickened into a fog that surrounded him. The air turned cold and damp; he shivered. His fly reel unwound completely, and the increasing force pulling it into the swirling vortex below him snatched the fly rod and reel from his grasp.

"My fishing rod!" he shouted.

The Holy Cross began circling in the vortex, and he immediately forgot about the rod when he realized he was in trouble.

The swirl spun even faster. The waterspout grew more intense, blowing fiercely against The Holy Cross and splashing waves over the boat's sides. Panic overtook David as he fumbled with the lanyard for the engine start switch, his hands sweaty and slipping.

He grabbed both sides of the boat to avoid falling overboard. The vortex's funnel now spun the boat completely around. He shouted for help, though he doubted anyone would hear him. All he could see were the walls of water rising higher. Panicking, he let out a scream that tore his throat.

Then the boat turned sideways, flipping David into the swirling water. He paddled with his arms to keep afloat and stop the current from pulling him under. An unfamiliar force jostled his body upright just as he had hoped. The experience felt like a merry-go-round without seats or horses. It might have been fun if it weren't so terrifying.

Then a strange shift in motion happened. The whirlwind started lifting David upward, away from the swirling whirlpool. The wind pushed him higher. The vortex of spinning white wind and water expanded as it pulled him even higher.

As he spun, he saw the outside of the swirling white-water wall. Around him was the creek and its banks. Below, his boat circled in the same counterclockwise direction he was spinning.

Then the vortex swallowed it. Maybe the vortex pulled it under, or maybe hurled it out. But why didn't the vortex pull him under or throw him out? And why did he stay upright—and move upward—without effort? David's fear eased slightly, and he began to enjoy this strange phenomenon.

And not just him—fish, turtles, frogs, shrimp, even a seagull spun with him in the now-large waterspout swirl. Maybe the old stories of frogs raining from the sky were true.

Then it happened. David felt fear and trembled.

***

At first, David thought he saw something red emerge from behind the white-water wall, but he wasn't sure. David clearly saw the swirling waterspout form and open up inside.

Oh Lord, what is that? The head and neck of a fiery red horse poked through the swirling mist of the vortex.

David yelled, "God help me." He wanted to close his eyes, but something wouldn't let him. Everything felt as if it were happening in slow motion.

The horse whinnied so loudly it rang in David's ears, and his hair stood on end as the sound echoed in long, flowing waves bouncing around the vortex. It was like trumpets announcing the arrival of cavalry.

The flaming horse's mane flickered with fiery red as it galloped, shooting smoke and fire from its nostrils while struggling to pull its body through the wall of white water in the waterspout.

A thunderous voice echoed, "Alastor, pull harder." Alastor strained his massive, fiery muscles. The air around him sizzled with heat. His eyes burned like fireballs, and smoke billowed from his nostrils. He slowly drew a two-wheeled, fiery chariot into the open whirlwind.

The charioteer resembled a man David might have envisioned in the Bible—tall, with a white beard, long, curly white hair flowing in the wind, black eyes, a flaming whip in one hand, and a scroll in the other. He wore a waistcoat and a breastplate strapped to his chest, with leather boots that reached just below his knees. Perhaps he was a warrior from some legendary tale.

With a crack of the fiery whip, the flaming horse and chariot slowly pulled up beside a frightened David, who floated in the middle of the spinning white-water wall.

Water stung his eyes as David blinked, but the man's gaze held him firmly.

"Get in!" the man ordered.

David hesitated. If this is God's answer to escape the whirlwind, I'll take it. He climbed into the chariot.

The strange chariot pilot shouted, "Alastor, up!"

The blazing red horse turned to face straight up toward the blue sky. David's knuckles turned white as he gripped the edge of the chariot, his stomach twisting. He looked down from the chariot and saw his boat, The Holy Cross, safely in Trent Creek; beyond it, the steeple of the old church rose. David wished he had gone to church.

"You won't need an earthly vessel where you're going." A shiver unrelated to the whirlwind ran down David's spine.

Huh? David asked, his eyes wide as he looked at the man.

They emerged from the top of the whirlwind with a thunderous blast that sounded like an airplane breaking the sound barrier. The sky shifted from partly cloudy to bright and sunny, yet David saw no sun. As the chariot left the whirlwind's funnel top, it leveled out, revealing a wide stretch of lush green grass and trees—quite different from the tree-lined creek bank. The chariot slowed down and settled onto the grass as if landing on a pillow.

The man grabbed David by the arm, and they stepped out of the fire chariot into a lush, solid, earthlike garden. Surrounded by green fruit trees, nut trees, and fields of colorful vegetables, the garden was breathtaking, with a clear river flowing through it, nourishing everything. The smell of the vegetable fields and various trees was heavenly to David.

With a whistle from the older man, Alastor and the flaming chariot took off and disappeared.

David stared, jaw dropping, eyes wide as he tried to process the unbelievable sight.

The man stood quietly while David stared in stunned silence. David shook his head and yawned, exhausted from the experience and a lack of sleep last night. He rubbed his hand over his face.

Are you feeling tired, young man?

"I think so. Not enough sleep." David sank onto the lush grass, feeling heavy.

The stranger chuckled softly, a deep, rolling sound. "Humans."

Don't you need to get some rest?

"No. People in my world don't need sleep."

David suspected the older man might be a bit senile or have dementia, yet he seemed quite clear-headed at the moment. Everything that was happening felt strange, but David knew he still needed to show his appreciation.

"Thank you for saving me from the waterspout. I would have died if you hadn't rescued me." The gentleman nodded, sat on a tree stump, and invited David to sit on the green grass in front of him.

"You're welcome. But what is a waterspout?" He tilted his head, his expression genuinely curious.

Ah! A chance to teach the older man about atmospheric phenomena. David launched into a detailed explanation of how waterspouts, dust devils, and hurricanes form. He exhausted himself trying to explain everything he knew about different kinds of storms.

The man's smile grew wider as he listened, then he slapped his knees, stood up, and burst into laughter.

"That was the best storytelling I've heard in years," the man said with a genuine smile.

David wagged his finger at the older man.

"Making fun of others is a sin," David said.

The older man stepped back. "Making fun?"

"No, I thought you were being funny," said the older gentleman.

The older man sat back down on the stump, folding his hands over his stomach as he continued to chuckle softly.

In a gentle, fatherly tone, he said, "You may need to get serious." He leaned forward slightly with a somber expression. David shot him a strange look.

When you see a whirlwind and a flaming chariot of fire, don't you think you should reflect on that?

"Meaning what?" David frowned, running a hand through his hair.

"Understanding what it all means and represents, that's all."

"I'm thinking about it."

The man stroked his beard. "And why I rescued you," he added after a pause. "I rescued you because you called out to God for help. You need to thank Him."

"Ah." David's gaze dropped back to the man, the serious expression fading away. David looked up. "Thank you, God." He smiled.

"Umm... I'm getting hungry," David said, embarrassed by how his request sounded. Do you know of somewhere we can get food?"

Thousands of years later, people are still the same. They still want food.

"Yes, I do," the old man grumbled.

"Follow me." The older man grunted as he pushed himself up from the stump and started walking into the woods.

They walked to a small creek. A sign on the bank read "Cherith." The older man reached into the shallow water and pulled out the biggest trout David had ever seen.

"How could you catch that fish with your hands?" David asked.

The older man shrugged, a smile playing on his lips.

Practice: A friend showed me how to catch fish.

David decided to look for firewood, and the man agreed to prepare the fish for their meal. As he walked away, a bolt of lightning, out of the clear sky, struck very close to the older man. David ran to him. The man stood there, holding a silver serving tray with cleaned, cooked, and ready-to-eat fish that mesmerized David.

How did you manage to do that?

The older man tilted his head toward the sky, pointing with a long finger, "A bolt of lightning fell from Heaven," he said matter-of-factly. "And a miracle happened."

Things gradually made less and less sense to David over time.

Many eons ago, I had divine fire to cook meat on a woodpile I had soaked in water.

David squinted, leaned in slightly, and looked suspiciously at the older man. "You think I tell stories," he said. He left it at that and sat down to enjoy the fish. After he finished eating, he grew very sleepy. The older man watched him.

***

David dreamed he saw Deacon Eddie pulling the ropes and ringing the heavy bells at the old church. David had never paid much attention to how frail Deacon Eddie looked. After years of faithful service, Deacon Eddie struggled to pull the ropes attached to the heavy church bells. David realized that he could have helped Deacon Eddie by ringing the bells.

Much later, David woke to something wet and rough licking his face. Its hot breath reeked. David shot upright, wiping his face with his sleeve. He opened his eyes to see a wide gray tongue slobbering from his chin, across his lips and nose, up to his hairline.

He screeched and jumped to his feet. He ran straight into the older man's belly and bounced off him like a ball.

The man laughed so hard he couldn't catch his breath. He leaned against a nearby tree, wiping tears from his eyes. After he recovered from his fit of laughter, David pointed at a lion sitting next to a lamb among a flock of sheep. "It's going to eat the lamb!"

"No, David," the older man said, placing a hand on David's shoulder. "The lion is tamed. He wouldn't hurt a lamb. All animals are peaceful in this place."

"How did you know my name?" David took a half step back, his eye twitching nervously.

The man shrugged. "You mentioned it."

"Told? Hmm . . . okay. How long did I sleep?" David rubbed his eyes; the world was still a blur.

I'm not certain.

Do you have a watch? You know, to tell time?

"We don't have watches or track time here; we don't need a sundial because our light doesn't come from the sun. We don't need to sleep here." The man pointed toward the sky with a peaceful smile.

David pinched his arm to ensure he was still alive. "Then tell me where this daylight comes from."

"From the Son of Man." The older man turned and walked away.

Despite how strange the entire experience was, some parts felt oddly familiar to David. David wondered where he was and how he could return home.

He followed the man as they strolled through a beautiful countryside, where green fields of various vegetables dotted the land, and beyond them, large mansions of different sizes, shapes, and styles rose.

David wondered why the roads all shone yellow, like gold. But he had a more important question. What is this place? Then he lost his nerve and wasn't sure he wanted the answer. He didn't get one.

"Just as well," David grunted.

As they walked silently together, David finally asked, "Could you take me back to my boat, The Holy Cross?" The older man stopped walking, planting his feet firmly on the golden road.

"Nope. Sorry. I can rescue people, but I can't take them back," he said. "That gate opens one way."

Fear slowly crept back into David's mind, and he started to panic. "My wife expects me to be home by dinner, and it must be about that time now because my stomach is growling like a lion."

The older man smiled and ran a hand through his long, white beard. "A man does not live by bread alone."

"What other principles does he live by?" David asked.

Instantly, David saw a vision of Mrs. Flora Mae hurriedly dressing her children for Sunday school, then gathering her teaching materials for the Primary Children's class. He had only now realized that Mrs. Flora Mae had sacrificed time with her own children to teach his children as well. Guilt weighed on his conscience. He needed to get to church and do his part—both for them and for Jesus. If he could return to church, he promised himself he would not complain about the boring preacher.

David begged the older man to take him back to his boat. He clasped his hands together, his voice trembling. His wife and children would worry themselves sick about him.

The older man stepped closer to David and placed his hand on David's shoulder. The touch was unexpectedly warm. "When you came, your sin breached heaven, and you must die before you can return to Earth."

David stared at the old man as tears welled up in his eyes. His children flashed through his mind, along with his beautiful wife and the sense of fulfillment from serving God in church.

Then he said, "I love my wife, my family, and my Savior. I will gladly die for them. Who or what is going to kill me?"

The older man pulled a two-edged sword from its sheath and held it high. The steel shimmered with a deadly shine.

"Please! I beg you— is there any other way?"

The man's eyes flashed bright red as he raised his hands and sword.

"Who are you?" David asked.

"Elijah."

The sword struck like a flash of red lightning.

For a moment, darkness and silence were all that existed.

Then David survived whatever it was he had just experienced. A cooler full of fish sat in front of him in the boat, and his fishing rod lay beside it. He checked his watch. "Ten minutes before Sunday worship starts."

He gunned the boat's motor and steered The Holy Cross toward the old church. He pictured Deacon Eddie's hands reaching for the bell ropes, but today I'll help him.

2

Chapter 2

"DANIEL'S LIONS"

When Daniel discovered his pet lion, Elmo, torn to pieces by the riverside, he stumbled back a step; he felt sick. A predator mauled Elmo's head, separating it from his shoulders. It ripped his body into four quarters. Something left claw marks and teeth marks on the severed parts. Daniel clenched his fist.

What animal could kill a lion? Daniel traced a claw mark on a nearby tree trunk, his jaw tight. Elmo was the king of the lions, and he did not take his own life.

Daniel whistled for the rest of his pet lions.

When Linus, Damien, Job, and Maze arrived, their reactions surprised Daniel. They smelled the mangled meat and blood, and then they entered into some ritual howling that Daniel had never heard before.

They pawed and clawed the ground, growling and snapping at each other. These lions were unique because God had shut their mouths in the lion's den and then made them Daniel's pets after his release. Somehow, they understood when Daniel instructed them to search along the river for clues of another animal.

Daniel wondered why Elmo was alone. He kicked at the dust near the riverside, dirt flying into the slow-moving water. He had never separated himself from the pride of lions before. But Daniel knew that their own desires could tempt, lure, and entice a person or a lion. That meant separation from the fellowship, which always brought trouble.

While walking along the banks of the Euphrates River in Babylon with the lions, Daniel tossed a loose rock into the murky water. He remembered the day his people arrived from Israel as captives. The entire nation had succumbed to temptation and sin, turning away from God. As a result, they faced only trouble. Everyone was worn out after two months of marching through the harsh desert and rocky, arid land. It was miserable, especially for the women and young children; their companions left others behind when they fell.

On the banks of the Euphrates River, their captors made them sing a song. They were exhausted, hungry, and in a foreign land. They did not want to sing, but they feared refusing and incurring deadly punishment. Daniel saw his mother's hand tremble as she reached for his.

The Babylonian conquerors were tolerant of relaxing music. They demonstrated their dominance by subduing captives and forcing them to sing. At that time, Daniel was a young boy sitting beside his mother when the Israelites started to sing. He fiddled with a loose thread on his tunic. The song they sang was so beautiful that even the birds stopped to listen.

It gave God's children an adrenaline rush. It strengthened them both spiritually and physically. God removed their past sins of pride and selfishness and transformed them—restoring their desire to survive and live. A man near Daniel openly wept, wiping tears from his face with a rough hand.

After seventy years of captivity, being thrown into a lion's den, starving, and enduring assimilation into Babylonian and now Medo-Persian society, Daniel was finally freed. But Daniel, now in his eighth decade, was too old to make the journey back to their beloved land of Israel. Daniel sighed.

He served King Darius well and brought the God of Israel into Babylonian society. King Darius trusted Daniel and made him a close adviser.

In Elmo's absence, Damien now takes the lead as the king of lions, guiding Daniel in their search. Linus and Job flanked Daniel on the left and right sides, while Maze guarded the rear as they moved forward. As they searched, Daniel sang the song the Israelites had sung, which uplifted them just as it had their ancestors.

Without warning, Damien stopped moving and crouched. He held his head stiff and straight as his neck hair stood up. He moaned softly, turned around, and pressed his body against Daniel's legs to prevent him from walking. Damien began gritting his teeth and growling as the other lions lined up in front of him. Daniel's back was to the river, with the lions arranged in a T formation in front of him.

Daniel was surprised by the lions' actions. It was the first time he had seen such a formal reaction from them. He prayed silently and asked God to reveal to him what the lions had said. Then he heard a faint, wispy voice that grew louder and clearer until it became a distinct lion's voice whispering in his mind.

Damien paced the small space in front of the other lions, his low growl a constant vibration in the air. "Boys, I'm scared. A scent from a track in the sand brought back a memory of a fear my father told me about in a story. A picture painted on King Darius's palace wall tells us the same story about an animal and describes the scent I smell."

Are you referring to the picture in the hallway leading to the great room? Linus shifted his weight, glancing back toward the palace as if the wall painting might appear through the river mist.

Damien pushed himself more against Daniel's legs. "Yes."

When they heard this, the lions let out a low growl and moved their heads from side to side.

"Come, see the track I found." The lions walked in a straight line a few feet from Daniel and circled the track in the sand. It was round and bigger than a lion's paw. The six claw prints on the front of the paw were twice the size of a lion's. Two smaller claws on each side of the paw and three claw prints on the back were about the same size as a lion's paw.

"This thing looks like a cat's paw, a dog's paw, and a lion's paw all put together," said Job.

Maze stepped back, wrinkling his nose. "The scent smells like the burnt flesh of a dog."

"How do we tell Daniel what this thing is?" Linus paced in a tight circle.

"Stay here, and I will bring Daniel to the paw print," Damien said. He looked pointedly at the others. "We will sniff at the print and claw the sand where we stand. Hopefully, he will figure out the print. He has seen the picture in the palace hall many times."

Damien went to Daniel, bit the cuff of Daniel's robe, and pulled him toward the paw print. Daniel never told Damien that he could hear their conversation. He followed Damien without resistance.

The lions did what they had previously discussed—sniffed the paw print and pawed at the sand. Daniel fell to his knees, bent over as they did, and sniffed the ground. He raised his head, wrinkled his nose, and shook his head, showing disdain for the smell.

Daniel said, "God help us, protect us from this beast of death and hell." Daniel made the sign of the cross over his chest, his hands trembling slightly. "Lord, help me tell them this is the paw of a 'Hellhound,' representing the devil in animal form."

At that moment, the lions jerked backward, howling and growling, showing they understood Daniel's words. They quickly guided Daniel back to his home. For the first time, the lions were afraid.

***

Throughout the night, Daniel fought against this fear because he knew that neither he nor the lions should fear the Hellhound, no matter how terrifying and powerful he was.

The next day, Daniel spoke to his lions, reminding them of who they were—lions with supernatural power. Then they went to the king's palace, where Daniel told King Darius about the Hellhound's existence.

King Darius was deeply upset and feared that the people of Babylon were in great danger. He wrung his hands, a clear sign of his anxiety. The old stories terrified the king—people being eaten, children kidnapped, pets killed, and fire destroying crops. And no one could stop the Hellhound.

Before Babylon was officially recognized as a city and kingdom, the mural in the great hall told the story of the Hellhound.

King Darius said, pointing a trembling finger at the massive mural covering the far wall. "The Hellhound stories have been painted and told for generations. They represent true stories."

Be calm, Your Majesty, and let me tell you a story an Israelite priest told me: There was a day when God's sons appeared before Him, and Satan came also. God asked him where he was coming from. Satan told Him he had been walking around the earth in every direction, seeking a soul to devour. It is Satan's plan against God to throw Him out of heaven in an attempt to destroy God's creation of His image.

"God challenged him to test his servant Job, a man made after God's image. Satan did everything he could except kill Job to get him to curse and turn away from God. Satan destroyed all his cattle, camels, and livestock. He destroyed Job's riches, leaving him a poor man. But Job would not curse God.

Satan then took all of Job's children and family away from him, but Job would not turn away from God. His friends told him he had to repent for some sin he had committed, but Job had not committed any sin. Finally, Satan gave Job a disease of boils, pain, and misery, but he would not turn away from God. Satan finally gave up. It was a test God allowed to test Job's faith.

King Darius leaned forward, his brow furrowed with genuine interest. "What happened to Job?" King Darius asked.

By His Word, God gave him new children and restored to Job double what he initially had.

The king nodded, a relieved smile finally spreading across his face.

My point is that Satan tempted and destroyed one of our own. And he is now testing my faith, our faith. Be warned that he might use our own desires or even our family and friends to challenge our faith.

Nothing will alter my friendship with you, Daniel.

Daniel's hands clenched into fists. I pray you are right, Your Majesty. But Satan has deceived and then killed my lion, Elmo, by the claws of the Hellhound. He slammed his palm onto the nearby stone table. I already desire revenge for his taking Elmo's life. And with my lions, we will track this Hellhound, even if it takes us into the gates of hell. He finally met the king's eyes, his expression grim. Faith in God is our protection.

***

The moon was full, and the night was silent—perfect for Satan to dance in the moonlight before dawn.

In the early morning, before the sun dispelled the darkness, Daniel and the lions awoke to the screams of people discovering their pets and livestock being attacked by the mystical Hellhound, as shown in a picture on the wall of the king's palace.

The hopeful heroes left the safety of Daniel's home, preparing for an encounter with the deadly, murderous Hellhound. The sun was rising, and soon its light would be in their eyes, giving the hound the element of surprise.

He is a coward, just like Satan, and will rarely confront his victims directly. His style involves lying, cheating, and attacking animals and people from behind.

The lions tracked the Hellhound's disgusting scent, which matched the sounds of people yelling. They planned to use the hound's attack method against him. They moved up behind the hound on a street called Straight, with the sun shining into his eyes. The hound always retreated toward the sun. The lions blocked his path, so he couldn't escape without passing through them. The Hellhound would have to fight to get away.

The lions arranged themselves in a diamond shape—Damien in front, Linus and Job flanking to the right and left, and Maze following behind. Leaving Daniel behind, they marched in cadence toward the evil demon, who held a blood-soaked sheep in his mouth.

After Damien roared a warning growl, the satanic demon dropped the sheep from his mouth. His eyes turned yellow, and he started to back up while scanning the road for an escape route. The Hellhound turned away from the lions to run, but the townspeople approached him with hoes, pitchforks, rakes—anything close to a weapon they could grab.

He lowered his ears and whimpered slightly. He began moving toward the lions with no escape, outnumbered and with nowhere to run. His yellow eyes started to glow and flicker as he picked up speed. The hump on his shoulders behind his neck grew larger, and the hairs on it stood up and bristled. His fangs flashed from his mouth. His long, black body shimmered as his muscles expanded.

Running faster and faster, he charged at the lions and then launched himself high into the air, trying to jump over them. But as he did, Maze met the hound midair and clamped his teeth on the back leg of the hound, causing both to tumble onto the road.

Remembering who they were and the power they had together and in service to their master, the lions lost all fear. Damien, Linus, and Job jumped into the melee, creating a ball of animals that rolled and bit, locked in deadly combat. Fur, skin, and blood exploded into the air—finally, a scream like a hurt woman's howled from the contorted ball of battling fur.

The Hellhound fought bravely for his life, but was no match for the lions. He started to surrender to their clawing and biting when Satan emerged from a nearby volcanic rock face.

With a wave of his hand, the lions were pushed back and scattered from the battle. The Hellhound limped past them and continued through the rock face with Satan following. But before he disappeared through the rock wall, Maze leaped, and in one last burst of fur and blood, ripped the hound's long black tail off his body. The Hellhound screeched, but he and Satan were so stunned by this act of bravado that Maze escaped before they could react.

Daniel said, "It's over, boys. Let's head home."

"Not so fast, Daniel."

Daniel shifted his gaze toward the voice.

Satan reemerged through the rock face. "It's not over. Now it's time for you and me to settle this."

Daniel fell to his knees, raised his hands to heaven, and said nothing. He stayed in this vulnerable position for several minutes. No matter how much Satan tried, he could not strike, move, or do anything to Daniel.

Then Daniel stood and faced his lions. "Come, it is my time to fight."

Satan retreated with Daniel and the lions in hot pursuit through the rocky face. They entered a small room, reminiscent of a church vestibule. A darkened glass wall separated them from a much larger room.

Daniel saw dark silhouettes of people walking around, their arms chained. He heard some people pleading for water, some cursing God, some praying for relief from the torment of fire and heat, and others pleading for forgiveness of their sins. It was a chamber of horror.

Satan appeared and stood before Daniel. "I will destroy you in this place of hell!"

"No, Satan, you will not. You are a liar. You were a liar from the beginning, and you are a liar now. Deception and fear are your weapons. But my weapon is the name and power of the Messiah of God. He is the sword of the Lord. And in his authority, I command you to be gone."

Satan fled from Daniel's presence.

The lions let out a roar.

Daniel turned to them. "My fellow servants of God, let us return home victorious." When they walked back through the rock into the town, they were greeted with cheers and praises to God.

Then the people started laughing. They pointed at Maze, who was still holding the Hellhound's tail in his mouth.

3

Chapter 3

"CHRISTMAS ORPHANS"

The city of Nazareth was deserted, with darkness covering most of the houses. Something had taken away the city's innocence, leaving its old homes behind.

Working in Nazareth for the first time, Odom thought the payoff could last him all year if he hit it big. He stopped at the edge of town, weighing his first choice: where to begin burglarizing houses. It was a thief's dream come true, but where had everyone gone?

The remaining leftovers of less reputable men gathered at the local pub. They called it the "Thieves' Den." They discussed the strange, foreboding quiet in the city and what the night might bring.

Odom spoke with the local bartender about a job, but the bartender refused to hire him. Odom was too young to work in the "Thieves Den."

"You're a teenager," he said, squinting. The upper-crust citizens of Nazareth thought Odom was too young to work at a place like the "Thieves Den."

The bartender's response offered a smooth way to gather strategic information for Odom's job search.

Well, sir, where can I find a job?

"I don't know," the bartender gruffed as he wiped down the bar.

Odom believed the bartender, a pigeon, would reveal the information needed to make his plan succeed.

"Sir, I am hungry, tired, and scared." He kicked at a loose floorboard. While traveling on Jericho Road, my parents died at the hands of a band of robbers. I escaped my demise only because my mother hid me in tall bulrushes by a nearby pond. I had to bury—" His voice trembled. Odom thought, "A few tears will open this door."

Odom cried, wiping his hand across his wet face, the tears hot against his skin.

"Alright, kid, don't cry!" The man's voice was firm.

Go to Straight Street, two blocks down, and ask people there for a handout or a job. That's where most of the wealthier folks live. However, I doubt many are home, since they've gone to their ancestral towns to participate in the census and pay their taxes.

If you don't get a job today, come back tonight. I'll provide you with a meal, a place to sleep, and pay you a little to sweep the floor at closing time.

"Thank you, sir!" Odom nodded, hope flickering in his heart.

Odom quickly surveyed the houses on Straight Street. Watching for signs of life or movement, he found the conditions ideal for burglarizing several of the homes on this street. Who would ever suspect a fifteen-year-old kid of doing such a thing?

On any row of homes, a skilled burglar begins with the house in the middle of the row. If successful, they expand outward from the center.

Wealthy individuals fear thieves and dislike nosy neighbors, so they often build walls around their homes for extra security. But a wall can also provide cover for a burglar.

Odom cautiously climbed over the backyard wall of a house. He looked at the back door, but something heavy inside prevented it from opening. He found a way inside through a window. To his surprise, there were no windows on the back of the house.

Slowly and cautiously, he walked the home's perimeter looking for a way to break in. The house must have valuables since it has no other entrances. Curiously, he found a trace of stone dust on the ground near the foundation. He suspected the homeowner might have built it as an emergency exit. For a professional burglar, it made a perfect entrance.

He wiggles a loose stone block and, sure enough, finds a hole. He squeezes through the stone foundation opening and ends up on the dirt floor of a bedroom.

In the faint glow from the smoldering hearth coals, Odom started searching, looking for money or anything of worth. But the sliding curtains that made up the bedroom's boundaries revealed nothing of value.

He moved to the semi-circular, stone-built hearth that encircled a half-fire ring in the living room. From Odom's experience, he knew people would hide money in the hearth's wall, low to the floor, to keep it safe from the flames and heat.

His experience paid off. Odom found what he was looking for. He immediately noticed an offset stone in the hearth wall. His heartbeat quickened as he started to remove the stone.

"There's nothing in it!" a voice, high and clear, spoke from the dark.

The voice frightened him so badly that he jumped backward, and — bang — he hit the wall. He fell forward, burying his face in the dirt floor while urinating in his pants.

"I told you!" Again, the voice spoke from the darkness.

Then Odom heard a child's laughter.

"Who said that?" He wiped dirt off his face with his shoulder, leaving a streak of grime.

A young girl stepped out from a shadowy corner of the room.

Urine dripped from Odom's pants as he got up.

"Sorry, I scared you. But at least you're dripping water on the dirt. It will dry up." She gestured vaguely at the expanding wet patch.

"You're crazy, little girl! What are you doing out here in the dark?"

"Same thing you're doing, except I beat you to the money. I've hit every house on this row already," she said with the voice of experience. She held up a small coin purse and shook it, the coins jingling merrily.

The little girl told Odom she had hidden a bag of money and valuables behind the house. Now, she's leaving to go to Bethlehem.

"Why," asked Odom.

There's more money down south, especially with all the people registering and paying their taxes. The world awaits me. I don't have time to deal with you.

The dirt-streaked little girl's professionalism amazed Odom, who asked, "May I go with you?"

"No! You'll hold me back."

Before Odom could say anything, she slipped away through the escape hole. He hesitated for a moment, then followed. To his surprise, when he emerged from the same hole, he saw a local elder, a night watchman, standing there. The little girl was nowhere to be seen.

***

After the night watchman accused him of burglary, Odom sat in jail. The watchman confined Odom in a cave used as a jail and covered the entrance with a large rock. Odom pushed against it, leaned on it, and tried to move it, but to no avail.

At midnight, without warning, the rock shifted just enough for him to slip through and escape. Odom bolted for his life. He ran blindly into the darkness and collided with the back of the donkey standing there. He bounced off the donkey's rear and hit the ground—splat.

"What a stupid thing to do." The little girl rolled up her rope from the stone the donkey pulled, nudging it open.

"Who said that?" he asked, rolling onto his knees.

"I did." The same little girl moved closer to Odom so he could see her. "We both need to leave now! The watchman will be looking for us."

Can I go with you now?

"Maybe we could help each other," she said.

They headed into the darkness, and Odom had no clue where to go. "How do you know which way to go?"

A farmer in Bethlehem gave me this small, flop-eared donkey. He bought it as a pet for his children, but they lost interest, so the farmer gave the donkey away. Bethlehem is the donkey's home, and he will lead us there.

***

They traveled through the night, maintaining a safe distance from Nazareth. The next day, they wandered around Jerusalem, staying away from the area because the risk of being caught was higher. The donkey didn't want to go there anyway, and they kept moving.

Almost to Bethlehem, they came across a group of shepherds talking among themselves and behaving strangely.

The girl looked at Odom and said, "We should find out what's going on."

Odom approached the men. "Greetings, has something happened in Bethlehem?"

We are heading into town to see the... "Christ Child," another interjected.

"What's that?" asked Odom.

We watched over our flocks at night when an angel of the Lord appeared, and God's glory shone around us like bright daylight. Then the angel told us not to be afraid. He brought good news to everyone. Tonight, a Savior is coming into the world in the City of David, right here in Bethlehem.

When the angel of the Lord left, a multitude of angels appeared and proclaimed peace to everyone. You should have been here; it was an amazing sight. So, we are going to worship Him.

"May we go with you?" the little girl asked.

What would your parents think about traveling with us?

We have no parents; they have passed away. She said, "It would be wonderful to have a family again."

The new ragtag group of thieves and shepherds soon encountered three well-dressed, handsome men, along with their entourage of servants and camels, traveling in the same direction. Wealthy people's fine linen made up their unusual-looking clothes, and their voices sounded very foreign.

Odom and the girl exchanged glances with each other and with the unfamiliar men. They had never seen people like these before. They wondered if the foreigners had loot to find.

Greetings! called one of the men.

They seemed friendly.

Huddling in a circle, the foreigners, shepherds, and two little thieves began talking to each other.

"What is your name, little girl?" asked one of the foreigners.

"Chaya."

All the foreigners smiled, but Chaya didn't understand why they reacted to her name that way.

In our country, your name means 'Beauty of the rising sun.' Our king's wife is named Chaya.

One of the shepherds asked, "Where do you come from, and why are you traveling to Bethlehem?" The man adjusted the heavy satchel on his shoulder.

We came from the East, beyond the great desert. In ancient writings, a prophecy is recorded that predicts a new star will rise in the sky, and its light will shine over a place called 'The City of David.' He paused, gazing at the faces of the shepherds. In that city, the star would shine on a manger holding the Savior of all humanity. When the star appeared, we followed its light.

Another added, "Your king informed us that this City of David goes by the name of Bethlehem. Our group bears gifts for the Messiah."

The third said, "We have met many people during our journey to this place and learned to speak a bit of your language. Where do you come from, and why are you here?"

"We are orphans," Chaya said. "Our parents died, and we have no family. We wander from place to place, living off other people's charity."

Odom shifted his weight from one foot to the other. "Well, not really," Odom chuckled to himself. He mumbled, glancing down at the dirt.

"If we could have a family again, that would be glorious," Chaya smiled.

The three foreigners observed them closely.

Odom said, "We met these shepherds who saw God's angels, and the angels told them the same story about a baby and the City of David. They invited us to come with them to see the Savior."

"Good!" The wise man clapped his hands together, his face lighting up. Everybody, join us as well. We will share experiences and enjoy some food together. Our people call us wise men, and we want to hear more about these angels.

***

As they kept walking to Bethlehem, Chaya said, "This is nice. It is just like a real family again."

"It is nice to have children in our little family," one of the foreign men smiled back.

As they arrived in Bethlehem, people gathered on the street as they passed the local inn. The wise men stopped their wagon and asked a bystander for the location of the animal stable.

A man pointed down the street. "The innkeeper just sent a man and his pregnant wife to the stable because there's no room left in the inn. It's too crowded anyway. And besides, a birth would make everyone in the inn unclean for a week. Crazy laws."

"Watch yourself!" his wife yelled.

He leaned in close to the wise man and whispered, "Probably a win-win for everyone. At least the stable's quiet." He snickered.

Chaya's donkey suddenly kicked up its heels in excitement, then bolted away.

"No!" Chaya shouted.

A wise man said, "She won't go far."

"She has my loot in the saddlebags," she said.

"What is loot?" asked the wise old man.

Umm... the donkey took off with my old clothes.

When they entered the stable, the starlight shone brightly from heaven onto the baby. The Christ Child lay in a manger, just as the angels had told the shepherds and the wise men. The animals lowered their heads in respect to the baby, and a deep sense of reverence spread among both men and beasts.

One by one, the wise men presented their gifts of honor to the baby's parents. As the solemn ceremony continued, Chaya wanted to offer something too, but then she saw her donkey beside her male friend. Chaya quietly retrieved the saddlebags. She returned with the loot in a bag and then stood beside Odom.

They stood there for a long time, among the elegant foreign wise men and the somewhat smelly shepherds. Something about the baby, the Messiah-to-be, touched everyone's hearts.

***

The pre-dawn sky brightened as the shepherds started to leave, praising God. With tears in her eyes, Chaya handed the bag of loot to Odom, and they shared a silent look.

Odom never spoke a word. He took Chaya's hand, and they quietly walked toward the manger. He glanced at Chaya, and she nodded. Together, they knelt before the Christ Child and presented their loot-filled treasure bag.

Chaya squeezed Odom's hand and prayed aloud, saying, "Forgive us, Lord, for our sins. You know who we are. We are alone and rejected in this old world. Odom and I need a family, Lord, to love and be loved."

They remained together as long as the wise men worshiped, conversed, and praised.

Finally, as dawn broke, they left the stables with the three wise men.

"Goodbye," Odom said, then kept walking.

One of the wise men asked, "Where are you headed?"

By now, Chaya was crying and couldn't say a word.

"We have nowhere to go," Odom said. "But we'll find somewhere."

"No!" objected a wise man.

Odom and Chaya stopped, and the other two wise men smiled.

We want children in our family, maybe a boy and a girl. We will even prepare an official adoption decree. Will you come with us to meet your new family in a different land?

Chaya asked, "May we bring my donkey and her friend?"

"You will have to buy the other donkey, properly, of course," Chaya insisted. The two donkeys, like husband and wife, came and stood beside Chaya and Odom.

The wise man said, "We shall do it."

Chaya smiled. "Where do we sign?"

4

Chapter 4

"THE DEATH ANGEL"

Something flashed in her view of Venus. The object completely blocked her vision and moved so fast it looked like just a blip. She looked away from the telescope to scan the nearby sky and rooftop for any big bird that might have flown by. She saw nothing.

What was that blip, and where did it go?

Lisa sat on a small bench, staring at the stars through her telescope. Every fifth grader would have dreamed of the night view from the top of the fifty-story Central Park apartment skyscraper.

Her mother and father oversaw the building's maintenance, and her two older brothers helped with the skyscraper's daily upkeep and operations.

Everyone always had work to do after school, but at night, Lisa could sneak to the top of the building to watch the sky. And she loved it.

Her classmates complained that she only talked about the stars lighting up the night sky. Tonight would tell a story they would never forget.

Lisa kept her telescope trained on Venus, Earth's closest planet. The beautiful shimmer of Venus never lost its charm, and aside from that, nothing moved in the vast emptiness of space. Then, it happened again.

Something flickered across her telescope lens for a second, and everything went black. For the second time, she looked away, scanning the rooftop for a bird or anything that might block her view.

What she saw terrified her so much that she nearly fainted. She was too scared to run, scream, or defend herself, fearing retribution for what she had seen.

A giant black bird with human hands at the ends of its wings perched on the safety rail just a few feet away, watching New York City.

Lisa's fear and instinct to run for her life grew stronger, but her curiosity about seeing a man and a bird together pushed her to investigate the strange creature. Was it in pain and needed help, or was it a mutant monster searching for food?

She might be the appetizer, but the birdman paid no attention to her. It gently fluttered its wings and didn't look threatening.

She hesitantly asked, "Who are you?"

The birdman slightly turned his head. "You see me?"

"You're right in front of me," Lisa said, pointing her finger at Birdman.

"You cannot see me. I am invisible," he said, stepping back onto the handrail.

Peekaboo, I see you. What type of batteries do you use?

Birdman faced Lisa.

She gasped. Birdman had no face, only two red eyes staring at her through his feathers.

What do you mean, batteries?

Your power source. Lisa leaned in, her expression filled with skepticism. "What gives you the power to be invisible?"

"God." Birdman's gaze stayed fixed on the sky.

He must be a puny God if I see you. She crossed her arms. You need a cloaking device to be invisible. Spaceships have them. The movies taught me that.

Birdman lifted the full-length black winged suit that attached to his shoulders and hands. Looking up at the sky, he started to murmur some gibberish. She assumed he was speaking like a bird.

Feathers covered his entire body, with the ones on his head forming a hood-like covering, similar to a black hoodie.

His torso revealed a muscular male chest. Feathers covered the rest of his body from his waist down, wrapping around his legs. The feathers tapered off at the top of his ankles, exposing feet with sharp, claw-like talons. Lisa had never seen such a costume.

***

After finishing his rambling, he told Lisa to be quiet and leave him alone. He turned his back on her and kept watching the big city.

"Well, you are rude." Lisa took a step closer, undeterred. "Is that how chickens treat their children?"

"Are you calling me a chicken?" He spun around, talons scraping the handrail.

"Looks like you have chicken feet to me." She met his glare evenly.

Birdman faced Lisa and explained that God had sent him to collect the souls of people who died in New York City that night. As their guardian angel, he gathered their souls as they ascended to Heaven and guided and protected them from Satan, stopping him from stealing their souls on the way.

"Show me." Lisa held out her hand, palm up, a confident challenge in her eyes.

"I do not have time to waste on a child's pretentious request," he said, turning his back and staring out into the city.

"What is your name?" Lisa took a small step back, her brow furrowed.

"Mashchith."

I've heard of angels Gabriel and Michael, but I've never heard of an angel named "Mackled," or whatever you said. She chewed on her lip, lost in thought.

Birdman explained that some people called him the angel of death, but he was not that kind of angel. He embodied God's love, manifesting it like an angel. His love alone kept the devil from harming anyone's soul.

People misunderstood his purpose, believing he took lives. Only God has the authority to decide life and death. He cared for and protected their souls with love until he brought them to Jesus in Heaven.

"It's Mashchith." He pinched the bridge of his nose in frustration. "Very well. Come, take my hand, and look at the building next to us. You will see a soul emerging from the top of the building. You and I will deliver that soul to

Saint Peter, the greeter at Heaven's gate."

"How long will that take? My bedtime is ten o'clock," she said, glancing at an imaginary watch on her wrist.

"How quickly can you wink your eye?"

Fast. Okay! Let's go!

"Watch and hold tight to my hand." He extended his hand patiently.

She hesitantly gripped his hand, and the feathers brushed against her.

As Mashchith predicted, a long white mist, shaped like a person, rose from the top of the next building.

"Ready?" Mashchith turned his head, his talons flexing slightly.

"Yes," Lisa nodded, with a determined expression on her face.

Together, they flew toward the misty figure. Mashchith gripped it with his large talons, and everything else became a blur.

***

They floated down to a landing zone as white as snow. Lisa couldn't feel her feet touch the ground. She knew this place wasn't New York City. It was glowing and sparkling, and everything felt alive.

Mashchith smiled and gestured around them with a massive wing. "Welcome to Heaven, young one."

Lisa stood in awe of the magnificent, massive structures before her. Light streamed through the walls to the outside, illuminating the area. The outer wall, probably two hundred feet tall, reminded her of a red jasper healing stone she had seen. Twelve layers of different colors, each bearing the name of one of the twelve apostles, formed the foundation supporting the vast wall.

She felt comfortable and, somehow, loved, immersed in the radiant, vibrant colors.

"Stay here until I return." Mashchith vanished.

Lisa's mouth hung open as she stared at the two-hundred-foot-tall gates of pearl standing wide open. She took a tentative step forward, then another. The open gates revealed the city's gold-glittering interior and its gold streets. People mingled and walked around, and everyone looked contagiously happy. Adults shook hands and laughed while children played games.

"Like what you see?" Startled, Lisa turned toward the voice. A man in a long, white robe, his white beard framing his face, stood before her.

She stuttered, "Y-yes!"

You are a lucky young woman. Few people besides Saint Paul have ever seen this sight. And God forbade him from speaking of it to anyone.

May I speak of it?

You might. But do you think anyone will believe you?

She shrugged, a small gesture, saying, "No."

Would you like an inside tour of Heaven?

"Yes! But . . . my bedtime is ten o'clock." She paused to think, her brow furrowing slightly. "I could come again sometime! Right now, I need to go home, or my mother will worry about me. Where did Mashchith go?"

He'll be back soon.

Sir, who are you?

"Peter." He smiled warmly, the white beard framing his friendly face.

Lisa quietly stood, images of Peter attempting to walk on water flashing through her mind. He noticed her intense expression and guessed the curious ten-year-old had more questions.

"Is something on your mind?" Peter tilted his head, his gaze gentle.

Yes. Why do people have to die?

That's a difficult question, but I believe that the pain felt from someone's death reflects how deeply they loved that person.

And from Heaven's perspective, people don't die so much as they receive an upgrade to new life. When God the Father decides when someone's time has come, He often assigns that person a specific role.

When that moment comes, God sends Mashchith to safely escort the person home to Heaven, ensuring no further harm befalls them. They will never die again.

Mashchith went back to Peter and Lisa, who were standing in front of Heaven's open gate.

"Are you ready to go back to your earthly home?" he asked Lisa.

Yes. I need to be home by my bedtime, or Mother will worry.

Lisa tugged at Mashchith's hand.

Hold my hand firmly.

"Will you take me to Venus and Mars so I can see them?" Lisa looked up at him, her eyes wide with anticipation.

Peter grinned.

Mashchith sighed. "Well... okay." He looked at Peter, who only smiled more warmly.

Goodbye, Mr. Peter! I really enjoyed talking with you.

Peter smiled and waved goodbye, and the two travelers then disappeared.

***

"Look, Mashchith! Isn't Venus beautiful?" Lisa pointed a small finger toward the planet. The yellow-white ball of Venus shone brightly and radiantly.

"What causes it to look yellow?" She squinted, trying to understand.

It combines blue and gold.

Lisa gasped and stared at the sight.

I am impressed by your curiosity. However, remember that beauty can be a deadly attraction. Venus has a poisonous atmosphere that contains carbon dioxide and sulfuric acid. If you, as a human, breathe it, it could kill you. Plus, the temperature on Venus is 900°F. You would roast before reaching the planet's surface. After all, it is the second planet from the sun.

Remember, how something looks, whether beautiful or not, isn't always good or bad. Always take the time to understand the person, place, or thing before making a judgment.

Lisa moved closer to Mashchith and looked at him. She tilted her head, her fear replaced by fascination. He smiled, and Lisa saw his mouth and smile for the first time. He didn't look dangerous to her. She wrapped her arms around him. "Thank you for bringing me here. You are not a death angel but an angel of love."

"Thank you for understanding." He hugged her back. "Now let's take you to Mars."

In an instant, they hovered over the planet Mars. To Lisa's astonishment, Mars appeared half the size of Earth and shone very brightly. "When I looked through my telescope at home, Mars always seemed huge, red, bright, and scary. The reddish color makes it ugly compared to Venus."

You are right, but you would weigh only a third of what you weigh on Earth, which would allow you to jump very high. Not everything about Mars is bad. However, the atmosphere here isn't breathable. And for a human, Mars can get very cold.

"Burr!" Lisa said, shivering and rubbing her arms.

Are you ready to go back home?

She nodded while biting her lip.

As they lifted, Mashchith became serious and quiet. He looked straight ahead, his expression unreadable.

Lisa prayed that nothing was wrong.

They suddenly appeared on the rooftop of her apartment building.

Let's take a moment to sit on your small bench.

They sat, and she looked at him intently. The night air lay calm around them, and the city lights hummed distantly below.

Lisa, you are exceptional. You demonstrate the kind of love that God the Father and His Son, Jesus, seek. That is why Jesus died. Your love and faith in Jesus will guide you until I come for you someday.

Lisa reached out a hand as if to stop him from leaving, then let it fall to her lap, her expression a blend of awe and sorrow.

She glanced and nodded.

You are young and should love, comfort, and support your family through both good and bad times. Helping your family and friends is another reason God the Father and Jesus let you see Heaven so that you would help them. When you get angry or feel hurt or sad, think about what you have seen and experienced tonight.

He met her eyes with such intensity that it took her breath away. "Okay." She looked down, then back at him. "Will you come back and talk with me sometime?" A small, sad smile touched her lips, then vanished as quickly as it came.

"Yes. And you may see me through your telescope as I pass by in the air." He looked at her with a hint of pain in his red eyes. "Enough of me. Your mother needs you." Mashchith stood, his form seeming to shimmer in the moonlight.

Lisa felt Mashchith's wings beat as he took off from the roof.

Just then, an elongated white mist appeared on the rooftop, taking on the shape of a person before slowly fading. Mashchith reached out and grasped it. His hand closed around the swirling mist, and then both vanished.

***

Lisa took the elevator down to the family apartment on the first floor. She stopped at the door's threshold, her heart pounding wildly against her ribs.

Her mother and two brothers sat on the couch, crying together and comforting each other. Tears rolled down their faces, silent streams of grief.

Lisa ran into her mother's open arms, crying. "What happened? What happened?"

"Your father had an accident tonight," she sobbed uncontrollably.

"An accident?" No one would cry out like that if someone were okay.

Her mother calmed down enough to say, "Your daddy died, sweetie."

"No! It can't be. No!"

Her brothers included Lisa in their group hug. Their warmth enveloped her, a fragile shield against reality.

Please tell me, Mama. What happened?

She repeated, "I don't know what we'll do. I don't know what we'll do." She rocked back and forth slightly, staring into space. Then she asked, "How can God be so cruel?" Her mother blocked her tears with her hands.

Joe told Lisa, "Dad had an emergency. An elevator had gotten stuck on the second floor with people inside." He paused and cried, wiping a shirt sleeve across his wet face.

That old elevator always struggled to reach the second floor. Dad, a certified elevator mechanic, would often go into the service area beneath the first floor to work on the hydraulic pumps.

Joe continued, "Normally, we would help him insert the safety poles under the elevator as a safeguard and watch out for him. For some reason, Dad told Jim and me to go to dinner, saying he had done the task a hundred times before and would be fine. He would meet us at dinner." Joe looked away, his voice catching.

Lisa looked at him. "And?"

Today, Dad didn't set up the safety poles. We don't understand why he didn't put the poles under the elevator.

A knock at the door, and their pastor entered. He comforted them and read from the Bible. Lisa moved to a chair as she recalled Mashchith's words.

After the pastor prayed, Joe handed him a cup of coffee as the man sat at the dining table.

Lisa sat beside her mother to comfort her. "Mama, I have something to tell you." She gently touched her mother's arm. Her mother looked at her with teary eyes.

The pain we feel is our way of showing love for Dad. And his passing was a new beginning. We'll see him again, so don't worry, Mama. Lisa kept her voice steady, even as tears filled her eyes.

Tonight, while I was on the roof, I saw Dad's soul rising to Heaven. God's angel came and took Dad home because Jesus had a special mission for him in Heaven. He is safe, and he will wait for us in Heaven.

Her mother hugged Lisa and said, "For a ten-year-old, you are wiser than your age. And you comfort me. Who told of such things?"

"Mashchith."

The pastor spilled his coffee on the floor, making a mess everywhere.

Lisa's mother stiffened and looked at the spilled coffee, then at the pastor.

"Something wrong, preacher?"

"Yes," the pastor said, his face wild and disturbed. "Do you know who Mashchith is?" Her mother said, "I don't believe I have ever heard of him. Is he a new tenant in the building?" The pastor had a wild, disturbed look. With trembling hands, he knelt beside Lisa.

How did you find out Mashchith's name?

He told me his name, and Lisa tilted her head with a look of confusion on her youthful face.

Lisa's mother nervously said, "For God's sake, Pastor, who is this Mashchith?"

That name belongs to God's angel of death.

Lisa's mother gasped.

"He is not an angel of death," Lisa protested. She slammed her hand on the table, rattling the teacups. "He is an angel of love, guiding souls to Heaven."

Everyone stared at her. A fork clattered onto a plate, the sound sharp in the silent room. "Before Dad died, Mashchith came and took me to Heaven because God wanted me to see so I could tell others."

Lisa leaned back in her chair, a peaceful smile on her face. I met Peter at the gates of Heaven and talked with him. He let me look inside, and I saw a big gold house and a gold street. People were walking around, very happy, and children of all colors played together.

The others nervously looked at each other, glancing back and forth. Jim cleared his throat, keeping his eyes on the floor.

Peter told me that God showed Saint Paul and me Heaven. He said I could tell anyone I wanted. He hoped people would believe that Jesus is waiting for us in Heaven. Mashchith brought me back to the rooftop, and I saw Dad come through the roof, where God's angel of love took Dad safely to Heaven.

Lisa's mother fainted and slumped onto Jim's shoulder. Jim flinched, struggling to support her.

The preacher sat stiff and pale as paint, his Bible lying forgotten in his lap.

Lisa wished Mashchith could join them so everyone could feel better. But she knew it would happen in time. She reached out her hand, longing to comfort her mother.

5

Chapter 5

"THE HOLE"

On the Appalachian Trail in the mountains of Western North Carolina, Marshall Doe was playing hide-and-seek with his twin granddaughters, Opel and Dora. They called him Papa. He closed his eyes and counted to twenty.

The girls ran off—and then stopped. Opel tugged on Dora's sleeve and pointed.

"Look, Papa!"

Marshall cut his count short and looked where the twins pointed. A flickering blue flame burned atop a boulder on a hill above the girls. He frowned, adjusting his glasses for a clearer view.

What the heck is that?

The burning blue flame fascinated Marshall, a retired government geologist who had never seen a phenomenon like it. He moved closer to the flame.

The flame flickered low, then higher, teasing Marshall into speculating that various pressures from some regulator controlled the beautiful royal blue color. It could be due to a natural-gas or mineral-gas exchange that no one had discovered.

He rubbed his chin stubble, excitement growing in his chest. The flame, so captivating in color and brightness, cast a spell on Marshall. He had to explore it further.

His granddaughters, curious but cautious, stayed back. The girls, frightened, clung to each other.

"Papa, it's like a ghost!" They watched their grandfather climb the hill to check out the flame. "Be careful, Papa!" they yelled.

Marshall climbed the hill, grunting and huffing, until he reached the fiery rock. He stood there, spellbound. His breath was heavy in his chest, and his eyes were wide at the unnatural sight. He ran his palm over the smooth, cool surface, which sent a chill down his spine.

He touched the large rock, and it felt cold—a strange trait for a fiery rock. The flame flickered steadily in blue, licking the air above the rock. Nothing else happened.

Then, the ground beneath Papa's feet trembled and collapsed. It swallowed him into a deep, hidden hole. The hole, just big enough for him, allowed Marshall to pass through as he fell.

Falling down the dark hole, he screamed for help, but it was useless. Marshall thought he felt things grabbing at him and touching him, and he heard faint voices whispering in the darkness as he kept falling.

Finally, he hit the bottom hard with a thud, splashing into water and mud. Without light in the hole, he couldn't see his hands in front of his face. But he could smell the gas rising from the splashed muck, and it sickened him. It reeked of rotting flesh. The stench nauseated him until he vomited, adding to the horrendous smell that only hell could produce. "Where am I? And what is this dark hole?" He wiped a sleeve across his mouth; his sleeve came away drenched in the stench.

"Yuck," he quipped.

He felt air pulsating on his neck as if someone had breathed on him. It stirred his fears, and goosebumps rose on his arms. No light, no phone, no way to contact his grandchildren. He could do nothing but hope they'd find help. He pressed his back against the damp wall, trying to enlarge the hole.

During a quick self-exam, he found no injuries except for something pressing against his lower back. His fingers brushed over a hard, rectangular object. The tight space prevented him from twisting or moving freely, but he still reached behind him. A shaft or stick protruded from the side of the hole, pressing into his back.

Marshall doubted he could escape and didn't know how to get out.

Fear and pity began to cloud his mind. He yelled again, but still no one responded. Marshall tried to climb the wall by digging his fingers into the soft soil and pulling himself upward. That effort loosened handfuls of wet, muddy soil from the wall.

He only heard the rush of blood in his ears, and his heart pounded like a jackhammer.

His emotions and nerves reached their peak. Before he realized it was a panic attack, he panicked and screamed. In desperation, he began to pray.

Lord, I know it's been a while since we talked, but I need help. I feel helpless, and I don't want to die in this hole. Please forgive me for my sins. Give me some light to see and lift me out of this darkness. Amen.

Then he added, "Amen. Amen. Amen." Maybe that would help the prayer.

He expected immediate results, but the darkness surrounding him remained unchanged.

Nothing occurred.

The object pressed more deeply into his lower back, increasing the pain. It felt like a warning of the hell to come.

He dug into the wall soil around his waist, making space to twist his torso and face the object pressing against him. He grasped and turned the object in the soft, damp soil, eventually pulling it out from the wall of mud.

Without light, he visualized the object by running his hands over it. It was about a foot long, rigid, and warm to the touch. Dimpled knobs capped the bone at each end of the shaft, with joints on both ends. His fingers traced the smooth, warm surface. Goose bumps rose on Marshall's arms.

Using his index finger and thumb, he measured the shaft's circumference, estimating it to be about the size of a broomstick. With a mental image of the object as a bone, he reasoned it must be part of an animal's skeleton.

Then a mystical hallucination emerged from the darkness.

A voice asked, "Why are you torturing me?" Marshall froze, his hand still gripping the bone, sweat pouring down his neck.

The voice paused. "Why can't you let my bones rest in peace? Are you going to beat me as my master did for doing something good?"

Marshall felt the tight space around him. His hope faded; no one else was in the hole. Where was the voice coming from?

Marshall asked, "What is your name?"

"Donkey."

Marshall muttered to himself, trying to rationalize that his mind was fooling him.

Donkey laughed at Marshall. He went honk, he went honk, he went honk!

Marshall's anger boiled over as he struck his fist against the dirt wall.

Who are you, and where are you based?

Your mind isn't fooling you. I am dead—I've been dead for ages.

It sounded like a donkey's voice. Marshall shook his head forcefully, trying to clear the noise.

I rested peacefully until you disturbed my bones.

Donkey recounted how Balak, king of Moab, paid Balaam, a pagan priest, to curse the children of Israel as they traveled toward the Promised Land.

To stop Balaam, an angel of the Lord stood on the road, ready to kill Balaam with a sword, but only visible to the donkey. The donkey turned away from the angel, thus saving Balaam. Balaam mercilessly beat the donkey for turning away from the path. The Lord allowed the donkey to speak and ask Balaam, "Why do you punish me?"

I'm talking to a fool. I know I'm crazy," he declared.

Donkey said, "The Holy Scriptures verify my story."

Marshall became furious and yelled at Donkey, "You're a dumb animal! God made man dominant over animals."

"I am Jenny, a female donkey, not a male jackass. I suggest you get a grip," Donkey yelled back.

"I'm sorry," Marshall said.

The donkey brayed, "He-honk, he-honk, he-honk."

The loud laughter angered Marshall once again.

How can I leave this place?

Donkey's face and head emerge from the dirt wall of the hole, shedding light inside. No doubt, you are an ugly donkey.

The donkey's head looked real as she moved her head at different angles.

Marshall reached out and touched her soft, velvety, long ear. He shook his head in disbelief.

"Please describe my face and head. I have never seen my face or head. My mother chose me over all her foals as the prettiest." Donkey nosed Marshall's shoulder, blinking her long eyelashes.

"Why should I describe you?" Marshall twisted his body, widening the hole.

"I haven't spoken to anyone in thousands of years. I would really appreciate a conversation." She gently nudged him again.

With Donkey's head held high, Marshall studied her face and then her profile from the front, her head raised and her face facing forward.

After a few moments of his murmuring, several grunts and ah-ha's, he looked at the Donkey with a deep, observant expression.

Well, about your mother, if donkeys are naturally ugly, I don't want to see the rest of your family.

Donkey nodded her head happily; she always knew what Marshall would say.

What features make me attractive?

Ah! Your donkey ears—no. Maybe your long muzzle—no. Those big, shiny white teeth—no. I know, those baby blue eyes and long eyelashes. I'll bet they've turned many guys' heads to look at you.

Donkey grinned, showing her big white teeth. She kept her ears upright and blinked her eyelashes. "How should I approach people?"

Back up to them.

Her ears drooped, she furrowed her brow, pushed her lips out, stared sternly at Marshall with one eye squinted, and said, "What do you mean by that?"

He felt bad that he had insulted Donkey, so he smiled. People like you because of your warm personality. Helping others is one of your personal goals, and your physical abilities are a gift from God. By backing up to people, you would help them mount you and ride safely to their destination.

Donkey's bubbly personality came back.

Now, how do I get out of this hole?

"You must climb out of the hole. Your curiosity got you into this hole, and your faith will get you out." She paused. "Climbing depends on faith. Yet you must also make the effort to climb. The evil in the hole will confront you. But faith brings wisdom, and wisdom reveals freedom."

Marshall struggled to understand what he just heard.

"Goodbye, Marshall." Donkey sank into the dirt wall.

Donkey's disappearance saddened Marshall; he wished she would come back. He enjoyed Donkey. She somehow made sense and gave him courage. He considered Donkey's conversations as answers to his prayers.

He weighed his options...

Well, follow what a donkey tells you.

Marshall was unsure how to escape the hole. He had nothing to grasp to pull himself up and nothing to stand on to push himself higher. He felt hopeless. His legs throbbed, and he couldn't relax them from the cramped standing position. He repeated Donkey's words, "Climbing depends on faith. You must also make the effort to climb."

He pulled his knees up, pressing them against the wall of the hole with his back against the opposite wall. His body and knees formed a perfect L-shaped wedge inside the wall. The wedge provided some relief from the leg cramps.

He realized that a crawling movement helped his body climb upward. Over time, Marshall began to scale the wall toward freedom. Wise advice from a donkey. He now reconsidered who he should blame for his own flaws. He grunted through the effort, his muscles protesting.

For the first time, hope gave him the courage to escape the hole. As he hurried up the wall, his confidence increased. Nothing could hold him back now.

Then a hand reached out from the wall and grabbed his forearm. He gasped, slipping on the muddy surface beneath his frantic feet. His hope faded. He paused his scrambling and entered a visionary state of mind.

He stood in the doorway of his bedroom at home, the room filled with beautiful women. Circling like a carousel, similar to a child's merry-go-round, they waved, inviting Marshall into his room.

First, he resisted by deliberately averting his gaze from the sensual, tempting display of the beautiful woman. Why are they in his bedroom? He looked again and now sensed their hands touching him. He experienced a strong urge to join them in their debauchery.

He closed his eyes, but that didn't erase the image or the sinful urge. His wife was with the women on the carousel. She invited him to join them.

"Why do you resist, my husband? You are in heaven. Come, enjoy yourself." His wife smiled, beckoning with a single slender finger.

Marshall jerked his head in refusal, but his eyes stayed fixed on her figure. He knew his wife would never suggest such a thing. His knees started to give in on the muddy wall. He dug his fingernails into the wet earth, searching for a grip. Afraid of slipping back to the bottom of the hole, Marshall cried out, "Jesus, help me!"

The hand coming out of the muddy wall kept grabbing his forearm.

A bright light burst inside the hole. Marshall saw the entire interior of the hole for the first time.

A man in casual, modern clothes, with short hair and sunglasses, approached Marshall and extended an oddly shaped ring. It looked like King David's six-pointed star but was different. Decorated with emeralds, rubies, and other precious stones along the edges, the star momentarily held his attention. Hesitant to accept the ring, Marshall paused, but the stylish man insisted.

He held the ring in his hands and examined it. A skilled jeweler had engraved Solomon's name in the center of the ring. The man said, "The archangel Michael gave the ring to King Solomon to capture Satan's demons."

Why are you giving me the ring?

The man asked, "You asked Jesus for help, didn't you?"

Marshall nodded.

The Father, Son, and Holy Ghost agreed they should offer help. The ring won't trap demons for you, but it will free you from their tricks if you refuse to surrender to evil.

Marshall held the ring tightly.

With Donkey's help and King Solomon's ring, you can defeat Satan's demons. Donkey will carry your burdens, and this holy ring, as your sword from the Lord, will strike down your demons.

The man began to fade when Marshall asked, "Who are you?"

"I am Gabriel, the messenger of God." Then, the hand let go of him.

Marshall kept shimmying up the wall of the hole. He moved closer to where enough light came through for him to see a clear plastic trash bag filled with what had to be millions of dollars. He grabbed a handful of the bills.

Instantly, Marshall slipped away from the wall and started to fall back down the hole.

But Donkey caught him on her back. Donkey commanded him, "Wear the ring and throw the money away."

As soon as he discarded the money and slid the ring onto his finger, Marshall began to rise again.

Tired and hungry, Marshall imagined a buffet filled with all his favorite foods. He started gorging himself on it. Once again, he began to fall.

Donkey caught him again. This time, Donkey said, "Repent of your gluttonous sin and remember the ring."

Marshall asked for forgiveness in the name of Jesus and felt the ring. Then, still on Donkey's back, he began to rise upward again.

Marshall saw the hole opening right above his head. He's almost there.

Then sickness overtook him, and he started to descend, slipping and slithering downward.

With no strength left, he surrendered and accepted that he would hit the bottom of the hole and die.

"Touch the ring," Donkey said.

Almost at the bottom of the hole, Marshall obeyed Donkey's encouragement for the third time and reached for the ring.

He slipped into a dreamlike state.

He feels himself rising and watches himself do it.

Suddenly, he reached the top of the hole.

He crawled out, and his waiting granddaughters hugged him.

Dora asked, "Grandpa, where did you get that beautiful ring?"

A new feeling of redemption swept through Marshall.

6

Chapter 6

"THE DEAD ONE LIVES"

Why would a child steal from the dead? Why would his parents allow Abiah's behavior? Abiah searched through the tombs and graves of wealthy people. Their markers were large carved stones bearing the family's name. Prominent and wealthy families often carved tombs out of rock, and Jerusalem had many to choose from.

If a tomb looked like a cave with an easy entrance, he would go inside and search for anything valuable. It was a unique way for a young boy to help his family earn money. The dead never complained, and it was exciting. You never knew what you might find, and Abiah always had a gift for special occasions.

Evening was the best time to start searching because most people were afraid to be in a graveyard at night. He mocked the day's rumors and stories. He couldn't believe the stupidity of people.

Woo-hoo! Who's going to save me from the devil and the depths of hell in the cemetery tonight? Abiah stuck out his tongue, crossed his eyes, and slobbered, giving a delusional look. "Oh! I'm scared."

He was eager to start digging up graves, so he began his search.

That Friday was terrible, based on what Abiah overheard in the market and on the streets. He had stayed away from everything. Now, Jerusalem was finally quiet. Suddenly, he heard people approaching.

Abiah hid as Joseph of Arimathea, a member of the Sanhedrin, and Nicodemus, a rabbi, approached a new tomb carved out of rock. Abiah recognized the two men from the Christian gathering he attended with his parents. They also held significant leadership roles in the community.

They escorted several servants carrying a body. The white linen wrapped around the dead man indicated that he was important and wealthy. They entered an open tomb whose entrance was hidden from Abiah's sight and hearing. He moved closer, sneaking between headstones and monuments toward the tomb's entrance, and hid behind a nearby small mausoleum. His heart pounded in his chest.

Abiah found this event strange. The sun was setting, and funerals usually finished by then. The gossip he heard suggested that someone might rise from the dead. Maybe they were doing some religious trick. He chewed on his lip, a nervous habit.

The men left the tomb and used all their strength to roll the stone across the entrance, but it was too heavy.

"All Hail!" The leader of a group of Roman soldiers placed a hand on his sword's hilt and stepped forward. "Is this the tomb of Jesus, King of the Jews?"

"Yes," said Joseph.

We will help you roll the stone over the entrance. Governor Pontius Pilate instructed us to guard this tomb from robbers for three days.

"Why would he do that?" asked Rabbi Nicodemus. He nervously looked up at the darkening sky, then back at the soldiers.

The chief priest and the Pharisees told the governor to put guards here for three days to prevent anyone from stealing Jesus's body. Jesus claimed he would rise again.

Rabbi Nicodemus said, "Jesus told them they could destroy the temple, but he would rebuild it in three days. Many of his disciples believe that Jesus spoke of himself."

The Roman captain raised an eyebrow. "You really think that, Rabbi?"

Nicodemus straightened his robe. "I'd rather not talk about it right now."

The soldiers pushed the stone over the tomb entrance. One soldier stepped forward with a pot of wax and a signet ring. The soldier pressed the governor's seal into the wax to prevent tampering. The captain examined the fresh seal with a stern nod.

Still hiding behind the mausoleum, Abiah covered his mouth to stifle his laughter. He shifted his weight from one cramped foot to the other. "This is the best trick I've seen. Wait till the soldiers open the cave, and nothing is inside."

Then the soldiers set up camp and prepared their dinner. The captain assigned four soldiers to be on watch that night and for the next day's shifts.

The soldiers surrounded Abiah's hiding spot, trapping him so he couldn't escape, so he hunkered down behind the mausoleum. If he moved, the soldiers would catch him and find out he was trying to rob graves. That could get him into a lot of trouble.

He grew hungry and worried that his mother would be angry if he were late for dinner. He picked at a loose thread on his tunic and waited until nightfall to try to escape. When he smelled the soldiers' food cooking, his stomach growled so loudly he froze, looking around nervously to see if anyone had heard.

Abiah devised a plan to steal from the soldiers while they ate. They sat on the ground to eat, so when they reached for water, they set their meal down, and he stole food from their plates. His plan worked perfectly. He clutched the warm bread to his chest, his heartbeat triumphant. The soldiers even distracted themselves long enough for Abiah to slip away and run home.

***

Saturday night, Abiah went grave hunting again. Curiosity drew him back to the tomb, guarded by Roman soldiers.

One soldier said, "If he comes out now, my spear will kill him again." He casually ran his thumb along the spear's sharp point. The rest of the soldiers laughed.

Abiah decided to wait until early Sunday to see if anything would happen. He quickly drifted off to sleep in his hiding spot.

He woke suddenly as the ground shook beneath and around him. He scrambled backward, pressing himself against the cold rock of his hiding spot.

After he regained consciousness, he saw a shocking sight. Something pushed the tombstone open. He looked around and saw the soldiers lying as if dead. Whether asleep or dead, he couldn't tell, but he walked among the soldiers, and no one reacted.

A light from the tomb drew him in. Abiah screamed when a man emerged from the tomb, climbed onto the circular stone, and sat on it. He wore white, and his entire appearance radiated the light of the sun. Abiah covered his eyes, the brightness almost too much to bear. This must be some dream or vision.

Abiah slapped himself to clear his head, but the luminous man still sat there.

He wondered if the person might be an angel, but he wasn't certain. Hesitantly, he took a step back, as the stranger's gaze stayed fixed on him.

The stranger spoke. "Abiah, don't you think your mother is worried about you?" A gentle smile touched his lips.

How do you know my name? Abiah asked.

I know everyone, the stranger replied. It's a divine thing.

You're an angel, right? Abiah whispered.

"Yes." The angel smiled with a peaceful expression that seemed to illuminate the surroundings.

What are you doing here? You should be in heaven.

The angel chuckled. "God sent me as an attendant to help his Son, Jesus, who has risen from the dead! And I'm to represent him to some ladies who will be coming. I rolled the stone back so everyone could see that Jesus had truly risen."

"For real?" Abiah's eyes widened in disbelief, and a flicker of hope flashed through his mind.

The angel nodded.

"I heard about that from my mother and father. They hoped he would rise again, but they doubted it. They think no dead man can come back to life. I think you're part of this lie or trick." Abiah crossed his arms.

Go ahead and tell them that Jesus is risen.

"No, I'm not going to lie to my parents." He shook his head stubbornly.

"Do you want to see Jesus? Would that help you believe?" The angel leaned in slightly, his gaze fixed on Abiah.

"Yes!" Yes!

"Do you know how to get on the road to Emmaus?" the angel pointed to a fork in the road.

Yes.

Hurry. You will see two men walking down that road. Then you'll see Jesus approach them. You can follow them and listen to what they say.

Abiah asked, "May I look inside Jesus's tomb before I go?"

The angel growled softly, stepping closer and filling the space with sudden, chilling authority. "There is nothing valuable in the tomb for you to steal." Abiah froze.

How do you know I was stealing?

The angel disappeared.

Abiah mumbled to himself, wiping a bead of sweat from his brow. "Chicken disappeared. He wants to keep the good stuff for himself."

Abiah looked into the empty tomb. The angel reappeared and pointed his finger away from it. Abiah ran out as fast as he could.

***

Winded, breathing heavily, and casting nervous glances over his shoulder, Abiah reached the road. He slowed to a hurried walk when he saw the two men ahead, heading toward Emmaus. He stayed close enough to hear them discussing the third day since Jesus's crucifixion.

Suddenly, Jesus appeared and approached the two men. He didn't reveal his identity to them, his gaze gentle as he asked what was making them so sad. The men exchanged a puzzled look.

They recounted the events of the past three days and how the chief priest and his followers had taken Jesus to the authorities, demanding that Jesus be crucified for false teachings. Jesus was a man of honor who had performed many miracles and presented himself as the Son of God. Both sides viewed Jesus's crucifixion as shameful.

The governor approved their request and ordered soldiers to crucify Jesus. It wasn't easy to watch. But he has risen, just as he said he would. The women who followed Jesus during his life confirmed his resurrection, and the men in their group also came forward to affirm it.

Jesus asked the men. His gaze was steady and focused. "Was it not told that Christ should suffer these things and enter into his glory?" Then he reminded them of Moses and all the prophets, as foretold.

They reached the end of their journey as night fell. They invited Jesus to stay with them overnight at their home.

Abiah followed them to the house and looked through the open window.

While dining with the strangers, Jesus took the bread, his hands moving with a familiar, deliberate grace. He blessed it, broke it, and gave it back to the men. When they received the blessed bread, God opened their eyes. Even Abiah could see the nail scars on Jesus's hands when he raised them and blessed the bread. It was Jesus, or was it? It must be some trick.

Then Jesus disappeared. Gone. Just like that.

***

Abiah was stunned to find himself in a second-floor meeting room, standing before a door marked "UPPER ROOM." He rubbed his eyes, feeling the rough fabric of his sleeve scrape his skin as he tried to clear the impossible vision. How he got there was anyone's guess. Was this a dream or magic? He pressed his hand against the cool, solid wood of the door, grounding himself in the physical reality of the moment. He couldn't figure it out.

Curiosity, or something similar, led Abiah to peer through the keyhole. He knelt, pressed his eye to the tiny opening, looked inside, and saw a group of men standing with Jesus. How did he get there? The same way Abiah did?

A tall, large man with a white beard said, "Thomas would not believe you appeared to us earlier. He told us, clenched his fists, "Unless I see nail marks in his hands and put my hand into the wound of Jesus's pierced side, I will not believe."

He couldn't believe a dead man could come back to life, yet there he stood—possibly—face-to-face with a man named Thomas. The man attended the same Christian gathering as Abiah's family. Abiah wanted to believe the impossible—that this man was the risen Jesus. Filled with awe by what he saw and heard, he kept peering through the keyhole.

Jesus stretched out his hands, palms up, toward the skeptical man. "Thomas, put your fingers here and feel my hands, and put your hand here and feel my wound. Have faith and believe it's me, Jesus."

Falling to his knees, tears streaming down his face, he said, "My Lord and my God."

Thomas, since you have seen me, you believe; however, others who haven't seen me believe in me by faith, and God blesses them.

A voice spoke from behind Abiah. A heavy hand rested on his shoulder, startling him. "What are you doing, you little booger? The stranger loomed over him. Your eavesdropping is going to get you in big trouble. I know your father and mother! They're looking for you everywhere. Go home, you little scamp!"

***

When Abiah got home, his mother hugged him tightly and thanked God that her son was safe. Then she scolded him for staying out all night and worrying his parents.

Abiah told her about his experience at the graveyard, on the road to Emmaus, and in the Upper Room. His mother wouldn't believe any of it. "Of all the excuses you've ever made, these are the craziest. Now go to your room and stay there until I call for you." She waved a dismissive hand.

His father, more mellow than Abiah's mother, suggested they shouldn't punish him for his excuses or whatever he may or may not have done. He called Abiah to come to them.

Abiah paused in the doorway. "Yes, sir. You called."

Your mother and I are not upset with you. When you didn't come home, we worried about your safety. However, some unusual things happened while you were gone. What you told us about your adventures is just as strange as what your mother and I have seen and heard. Follow us, and we'll show you what we mean.

***

When they arrived at the Jerusalem cemetery, Abiah asked, "Father, what are all these people doing walking around in the graveyard?" His father paused, a somber look on his face.

They are searching for their loved ones who the cemetery workers buried here.

"But Father, why are they digging up the bodies? Nothing's left of the dead except bones and the trinkets the family gave them."

His father smiled. "They are not after trinkets."

He kicked a rock and said, "I don't understand."

After Jesus rose from the tomb, saints who had long since died emerged from their graves and appeared to many in Jerusalem. The prophet Isaiah predicted it.

Abiah furrowed his eyebrows in skepticism. He looked at the busy crowd, then back at his father, with a mix of fear and disbelief on his face.

Look, Abiah! There is Joseph's tomb, empty too. This is where we buried our neighbor. God has opened all the graves in the cemetery. Our loved ones who passed away before us have come out of their graves, just like Jesus did.

"Where did they go?" Abiah shielded his eyes from the sun, his brow furrowed.

We're unsure, but if the prophet Isaiah is right, Jesus will take them to heaven.

Dad, I can't believe all of this.

Abiah couldn't resist searching for something the saints had left behind.

***

Forty days later, Abiah asked, "Father, where are the people going?" He pointed toward the procession in the distance.

I'm unsure. Let's follow them.

Jesus's disciples guided the crowd toward the Mount of Olives, crossing the Kidron Valley east of Jerusalem. Soon, Abiah and his father arrived. Jesus stood on a rock, addressing his disciples.

Jesus gave his disciples a command: "Go, make disciples of all nations, baptizing them in the name of the Father and of the Son and of the Holy Spirit. Then teach them to observe all that I have commanded you. And behold, I am with you always, even to the end of the age." He looked directly at Peter as he spoke.

Abiah couldn't help but scan the people around him, all wearing heavy jewelry. Jewelry like wristbands, earrings, and necklaces often fell off in crowds.

Seeing Rabbi Nicodemus and Joseph of Arimathea standing before the crowd surprised him. They caught Abiah's eye and raised their hands toward heaven, glorifying Jesus as the Son of God, the Messiah.

In the middle of the crowd, the men and others from Emmaus cried out and shouted, "Lord of Lords, King of Kings lives!"

Abiah nearly fainted when he saw the Roman captain and his soldiers waving their hands toward heaven and shouting, "Savior, Savior!"

The apostles stood at Jesus' right side, their hands raised to heaven, shouting praises to God for His Son, Jesus. "He lives!"

Abiah's parents raised their hands to heaven, shouting, "Savior, Savior!"

Everyone raised their hands in praise, exclaiming, "Jesus!" "Glory to God in the highest, for his Son Jesus lives!"

Someone nudged Abiah into the crowd. He turned to see the angel who had sat on the rock, then pointed his finger.

Abiah, will you confess your sins of theft and grave robbing? Do you want to be saved by grace and believe that Jesus will forgive and save you? He loves you, Abiah. Don't you want to inherit heaven and receive eternal life? Look at Jesus, Abiah. His hands are reaching out to you, and he's gazing at you. Come home.

A warmth of love flooded Abiah's body and soul. This emotional and spiritual experience, unlike anything he had ever felt, touched him and moved him to accept Jesus's invitation of salvation.

Abiah raised his hands toward heaven as tears ran down his face, shouting, "Jesus, my Lord and Savior, forgive me."

Suddenly, Jesus lifted off the ground! He continued ascending into the sky, and then he disappeared into a cloud out of their sight.

Abiah said, "The dead don't come back through monuments and trinkets.
They live through the risen Jesus. . . . And so do I."

7

Chapter 7

"BABEL"

"Is this my father?"

"Yes," she said. "He is not coming home tonight."

Gershom stood beside his mother, who knelt beside his father, Adir's, body. Nearby, two workers dug a hole in the sand and clay.

How can you be certain? I don't.

Gavriella cried out from deep inside. Tears ran down her face, and then a hand touched her shoulder. She looked up to see who it was.

A giant man wearing a gray tunic stood there, with a large sword in the sheath on his belt and a spear in his hand. "May I assist you and the boy, ma'am?"

A messenger from Babylon called me to come quickly to the tower. I didn't understand why until I saw my dead husband, and these were the men digging the hole.

The two men paused their work. One said, "Adir, a good worker, represented his grandfather Shem's tribe most admirably. This morning, he stood on top of the tower, measuring the cubic feet needed to reach the clouds. For some unknown reason, the wind suddenly increased and swept him from the top as if a hand had swatted him off. He fell about three hundred feet from the top."

The first man seemed unable to speak anymore, so the second one said, "We stopped working to have a moment of silent respect for Adir. We summoned

Gavriella and you, sir. We remained safe."

But not Adir. An insult to one of the Gods caused this accident.

Gavriella and Gershom cried as the others stayed still.

Ma'am, if you want the body, take it. But when someone dies on this job, we bury them in sight of the tower. We offer this burial as a free service; you can choose whether to accept it.

She nodded and motioned for the diggers to keep going.

"How old are you, boy?"

"Twenty."

Good! You're of adult age. You must stay and take your father's place. You will represent Shem's tribe as your father did.

Gavriella raised her hand. "No! Y-You—"

I will fill in for Mother—Father. Father would be proud of me.

***

Gershon worked tirelessly from sunrise to sunset. He struggled to grease the slide and move the rock blocks. Every day, blisters formed on his hands, and his skin began to tear. The taskmaster's whip, which pushed him to work faster, left scars on his back.

He worked at the tower, ate meals there, and slept with the camels at night to stay warm. He could only see his mother on the Sabbath, when everyone stopped working to worship the Babylonian god Marduk all day.

But Gershom's mother taught him to worship Great Grandfather Noah's God at home on the Sabbath. So, they prayed together at home to the God of Noah, asking for help to ease Gershom's burden of building a tower to heaven called Marduk. They base their faith on the existence of the invisible God—the God of humanity.

They could only seek and trust. And they did.

***

Gershom's only friend at work was Ariella. She managed to bring him buckets of grease to lubricate the slide. They often talked about the God of Noah and shared their deepest secrets and desires.

Her golden hair gently swayed with each of her steps. Her eyes, slightly slanted like a half-moon, highlighted the beauty of her dark brown eyes whenever she looked at Gershom. Gershom appreciated her tender smile and the gentle touch of her hand on his shoulder when he was troubled. He could listen to her soothing voice for hours. When she was gone, he pictured her.

When the stripes from the taskmaster's whip were bloody and painful, she applied some grease to his back to ease the pain and promote healing of the torn skin. Sometimes, she would make small corn cakes at home and share them with him during lunch break.

They were the first to arrive at work each morning, sharing their thoughts and hopes for their future together. One of the things that bonded them was that both had lost their fathers to the work of building the tower to heaven.

But their unity would not withstand a stronger force.

***

On the morning of the first day of the week, Gershom left his mother's house, eager to see his love, Ariella. He imagined what he might say to her, or she might say to him that day.

As he grew nearer the tower, he heard people shouting at each other. Some men were even fist-fighting, and others wrestled in the dirt. The competitors snarled at one another, showing no friendliness. Some faces bled, some screamed in pain, and lay in the dirt, and some pointed fingers at each other with weapons in hand.

Gershom came to a stop. His mind couldn't comprehend such a thing happening.

Mass confusion spread before him. Some coworkers spoke words he didn't understand. He saw his taskmaster and went to ask what had happened. The man started yelling at him in a language he had never heard before.

The taskmaster didn't bother chasing him as he ran off.

Gershom didn't know what to do, but he had to find Ariella. He pushed through the chaos of scared and angry people. He searched repeatedly but didn't see Ariella anywhere. He shouted her name until he could barely speak. Some people who understood him couldn't help because they were also calling out names as they searched the crowd.

Finally, people began gathering with others they could understand. Large groups speaking the same language started leaving the tower in different directions. Gershom sat on a stone block and prayed to the God of Noah. He asked for help to understand what was happening. But mostly, he prayed for guidance to find Ariella.

He sat on the block for a long time while others ignored him.

Then his mother appeared. She kissed him, hugged him, and thanked God for his safety. They were both relieved to be able to communicate in the same language. Then she led him to a gathering of others who also spoke their language.

The group talked for several hours. Some made plans to move on and find others who spoke their language. Others decided to stay and solve the mystery of the sudden language barriers. Still, some became so frightened that they lost their desire to live.

Several people asked Gershom for advice about his plans and what he would recommend they do. He spoke wisely, attracting others to seek his guidance.

Gavriella watched him. Then she moved closer and said, "God is preparing you to be a leader."

"But, mother, I am young."

Yes, you are, but your great-grandfather's brother Japheth had an ancestor named Enos, who was also young and served God when God called him.

Gershom and his mother prayed to God about the matter, then they stepped onto a stone block and gestured for the crowd to gather. The group grew bigger. Gershom introduced himself and his mother and briefly shared his family's genealogy.

Then he said, "I have a plan. We will split into three smaller groups: surviving, governance, and searching for the missing. Once we are organized into our groups, we will meet the next day to record everyone's name in each group. In two days, we will report our plans for survival, governance, and search efforts. Once we agree on these three plans, we will put them into action to reach our goals."

Finally, we must pray and trust in our grandfather's God, as the story of Noah shows, to guide and protect us during these difficult times.

***

Two days later, the entire assembly voted to designate him as the Head Shepherd of all people and groups. He hesitantly accepted the role, but his disappointment prevented him from searching for Ariella.

Every day, he ascended the unfinished tower to pray to the God of Noah and scan the landscape, hoping to spot a traveler or a sign of Ariella's return.

Whenever the divisions reported, Gershom found their reports boring. After such extraordinary changes in their lives, they remained ordinary people, doing everyday tasks. At each meeting, Gershom asked the search reporters if they had found blond-haired people. No was always the answer.

He grew restless, staying awake at night and climbing the tower in the dark to sit at the top, gazing east toward the route scouts had seen Ariella's family traveling.

Gavriella pointed out the obvious, "You are more depressed each day. Now I'm sad too." She gently turned his face to look into his eyes. "But you must admit what the rest of us have. The God of Noah decided that the people had to scatter. And he confused our languages to keep us forever apart."

Gershom averted his face.

She raised her hand and turned his face toward her. "Ariella will not come back to you. She cannot."

He grimaced.

"Stop longing. Stop looking," she said.

Gershom wept with a fury that nearly turned into rage. He despised those who forced his people and others to build the tower. He hated the God of Noah, who had punished him through Ariella's loss because of the arrogance of those in power.

***

The next day, he turned twenty-one but felt much older. That day, Gavriella introduced Gershom to three men who had proven themselves as leaders of their respective groups. He called them the rim of leaders; they would govern within their groups and ease the burden of decision-making. No one objected, and he agreed.

Then, he retreated into himself at the top of the tower. Again. The longer he sat there, the more he felt the tower itself—the whole idea of it—was cursed by him.

He wanted to die. However, Ariella's memory kept him alive.

Then he thought to himself, "The God of Noah is great. Greater than all others. Could he be greater than the curse he placed on the people? And if he is, could his greatness include any mercy? Mercy to the people? Or perhaps mercy to Ariella and me?"

He could only find one way. So he began to pray, hoping the God of Noah would show him mercy. He wouldn't just plead for mercy; after all, he was a leader. He intended to find this mercy and take it.

Sitting alone on top of the tower one evening at dusk, he saw a wisp of dust rise from the horizon. Excitement surged through him at the first sight of a rider coming with news, perhaps about his love, Ariella. His enthusiasm faded when the camel rider displayed the colors of another unknown group's flag.

The city guards couldn't understand the stranger's language. Frustrated by his inability to comprehend, they started pointing and gesturing for him to leave. The stranger resisted, pointing and shouting at Gershom, who was sitting on the unfinished tower.

Gershom stepped back and bowed to the stranger. He gestured for the stranger to sit with him.

He quickly interpreted the man's hand gestures to understand he was thirsty and hungry. Gershom ordered the guards to feed him. After the meal, the stranger took a stick and drew pictures on the ground. After some bargaining and hand signals, Gershom confirmed that the stranger wanted him to go somewhere with him, specifically toward the east.

But Gershom grew very suspicious of traveling with the stranger. Then the stranger went to his camel and retrieved something from the saddlebags. With his fist closed, he offered the object to Gershom. When Gershom accepted it by opening his hand, the stranger gave him a golden hair ringlet. Gershom sat down on the rock and nearly fainted from surprise and excitement.

After regaining his composure, he suggested they sleep and leave the next day. The guards objected to his plans because Gershom was their leader and had responsibilities to fulfill. However, Gershom convinced the guards to inform his mother and the rim leaders that he would return.

This hair is a sign. Gershom was sure. He would find the God of Noah's mercy, and he would grasp it.

***

The stranger led Gershom to a group of blond-haired people with half-moon eyes, but Ariella was no longer there. She and her parents had moved on, but she had told them about Gershom and left a lock of her hair as proof. They sent the hair to Gershom. The only problem was that they didn't know where she had gone, but the search team would continue looking for her.

Gershom returned a month later, dejected.

Gershom sat alone atop the tower. He ate his meals while sitting, observing, searching, and praying. Sometimes, he even slept on the rocks he had piled up.

"Where is the God of Noah?" Gershom asked aloud. "He has no mercy."

For days at a time, he sat and hoped. His faith in prayer diminished. His hair and beard grew long. Where is this God of Noah? This belief in an invisible God, without evidence, feels unrealistic.

***

At his most vulnerable moment, in the cold of winter, a lone camel and rider racing at full speed appeared on the horizon. The rider looked different from the others they had seen.

Gershom paid close attention to the rider. The rider was smaller than a man, and the scarf covering the rider's face revealed a bit of golden hair flowing in the wind behind them. Gershom nearly fell off the tower.

The camel kept charging full speed toward the tower, and Gershom ran down to the bottom. The hooves of the camel clopped loudly on the dirt, and Gershom wondered if his heart was pounding as loudly as the camel's hooves.

He reached the bottom of the tower as people shouted, "She has come back! She has come back!" and hurried to see if it was really her.

More people arrived as the rider approached Gershom. Before the camel stopped, the rider jumped off with arms outstretched and ran toward Gershom.

Her half-moon eyes and tender smile. Mercy had come to him through Ariella.

8

Chapter 8

"HELL'S WAR"

Satan always had hidden motives, and this moment was no different. He asked to appear before God in heaven. The tongue-flicking, lying, excommunicated serpent slithered to the foot of God's throne. Satan coiled up and raised his head.

"The prodigal son returns to the crime scene," God said. "But I warn you, don't raise your head too high."

Satan instinctively lowered his head.

"Get right to the point and state your purpose. What treachery are you planning?"

He tried to hide a sneer as his coils tightened. "Release my angels from their cells and chains, that I may commune with them."

"Denied!" God declared with unwavering authority.

Satan flinched, and believers were reminded of His supreme power and the security found in His sovereignty.

"Why do you punish them to hurt me?" the Devil asked, trying to look offended.

With a voice like thunder that shook heaven, God spoke. Satan trembled and quickly bowed his head.

God responded, "They were your advisers in your first evil attempt to overthrow my kingdom. They lost. You can do no more than I permit."

"You leave me no choice," Satan spat out, his demeanor suddenly turning cruel. "I wanted to avoid another war with you, but you show me no respect." The throne room darkened except for God's glory.

"I will continue to attack your pitiful humanity, and I will destroy your army of believers filled with your Holy Spirit. I already fight for their souls and have my own army."

"I am the prince and power of the air. I will free my friends from their hell-cells. If it means destroying the earth and your images, I will do it!"

Before you go, Satan, do you know Bert and Susan, who live near Black Mountain?

Satan's eyes narrowed, his tongue flicking in sudden curiosity. He answered, "Yes!"

"Why don't you try turning them away from their salvation? Since you could not take Job from me, perhaps you will find them easier prey," God mused. "If it were me, I would tempt them to sin against my Word. Then you could capture them for ransom. But, as in Job's case, you cannot kill them."

"Here's a secret for you: Susan is pregnant but doesn't know it yet. I granted her request to have a child, but you can't tell her."

"You treasure a prize, Lucifer. Consider: her child might also be another child of God."

Satan bared his fangs in a silent snarl, his hiss echoing as he retreated.

***

Bert and Susan never thought that digging in the dirt could someday change the world. Black Mountain was the ideal location for a below-ground storage cellar. Beneath their kitchen, they dug out loads of dirt, one load at a time.

Suddenly, a white flash visible through the small vents in the house's stone foundation illuminated their surroundings.

Susan stiffened. "What was that?"

"I don't know," Bert said. "Let me check."

He climbed the ladder to the kitchen when a sudden gust of wind shook the house. The jolt knocked him and the ladder to the cellar floor. The power went out, plunging the house into darkness. A faint yellow light peeked through the foundation vents.

"Are you okay?" Susan asked.

"I think so," Bert replied, blinking grit from his eyes and trying to regain his composure.

The mountainside trembled. Rocks and boulders loosened and rolled down the hill, crashing into the back of the couple's house. The impact broke the house's foundation; a wall and part of the roof caved in. Suddenly, everything went dark.

"What's happening?" Susan cried out.

"I have no idea," Bert murmured shakily. "Hold on to me, and let's feel for the ladder. Here it is. Help me stand it back up, and let's get out of this house before anything else falls and buries us."

They climbed the ladder and entered their kitchen. To their surprise, the sunlight flickered with a yellow hue.

"This isn't right," Bert said. "It's in the afternoon."

The couple exited the kitchen through its back door, one of the few things still intact. As they looked around the yard, they saw numerous mushroom-shaped clouds rising above the mountain peaks on the horizon.

"Lord, what kind of clouds are those?" Bert asked.

"Uhhh...who—what—is that coming toward us?" Susan asked, staring ahead in disbelief.

A figure approached, clad in armor that seemed both ancient and futuristic.

"Run back into the hole!" he shouted to the confused couple. "And don't come out until I come for you! A thermal fire is coming, and I will fight against it to protect you."

Bert and Susan didn't need any convincing. They hurried back into the storage cellar and hugged each other tightly as they sat on the dirt floor in the darkness. Bert couldn't think of one comforting thing to say. Susan whimpered, and Bert held her tight.

"Honey, please tell me what's going on," she whispered.

"I wish I knew!" Bert exclaimed.

What were those mushroom clouds we saw, Bert?

He hesitated to say it, but if the stranger is right, fire could hit their house at any moment.

"Did you see the neighbor's house?"

"Yes, I did," Bert said sadly, shaking his head. He was glad the darkness hid his worried expression from Susan.

Something tore it apart; do you think anyone survived, Bert?

Before Bert could respond, the wind hit the house again. This time, however, it caused no damage. Suddenly, the couple smelled burning paint and heard crackling wood.

"Our house is on fire!" Susan yelled. "What are we going to do?"

"We are doing nothing. The fire and heat will rise, and we will stay unharmed."

"Who was that strange man?" Susan asked again.

I have no idea. Just hold me tight. Maybe he will follow through on what he said and come for us. Until he comes back—if he does—I think we should pray for safety.

"Why?" asked Susan.

"If my guess is right, I think we're experiencing a nuclear attack," Bert told his wife.

***

Susan started coughing and gasping as smoke filled the basement. Bert gave her his T-shirt, and she wrapped it around her head and face. The shirt helped filter some of the smoke and ash, making it easier for her to breathe.

The two sat silently in darkness, holding each other and praying to God for help. Time seemed to stand still for them. Susan wished they had never dug the hole; it now felt like a grave.

Bert strained his ears, trying to hear something. Yet, there was not a sound.

"Babe, listen. It's quiet now."

No wind, no crackling of burning wood; the smoke and heat had dissipated.

"Who was that man, Bert, and what was he wearing?"

I have no clue who he was, and those clothes he wore... well, I have no idea.

"Honey, I think I might know who he is."

"Really? Who exactly?"

"The angel of the Lord," Susan said softly.

Babe, that's just nonsense.

"Who else could fight against fire and wind except an angel?" she insisted.

Bert fell silent and considered her hunch in his mind.

The cellar began to glow brighter as they heard someone walking across the kitchen floor toward the entrance. When the creature descended the ladder, the light it cast momentarily blinded Bert and Susan.

Eventually, the light faded, and a figure started to form before their eyes—the stranger who had appeared earlier, now in warrior's clothing.

Don't be afraid. God sent me to protect you.

"Were you at Jericho when the walls fell?" Susan suddenly asked.

Yes. You must be a student of the Holy Scriptures.

Bert furrowed his brow in surprise.

"I told you it was him, Bert."

My name is Michael. I am the Lord's archangel and lead God's army of angels. We are at war with Satan and his angels on this earth and inside the planet.

We previously cast Satan and a third of his angels out of heaven. God chained the worst of Satan's angels in the deepest pit to await the day of judgment.

But Satan has conspired to free his angels from their hellish cells and chains. First, Satan tempts humanity to destroy itself by exploiting pride, power, and prejudices, causing devastation to the human soul.

Then, Earth's people launch their atomic bombs against each other to bring about the worst physical destruction. The destruction of the earth weakens the human Holy Spirit's ability to resist Satan. One's faith is greater than any bomb, but the attack on people's flesh weakens their faith. This is Satan's only chance to win.

Humans are God's army. When people believe in and are saved by God's grace through faith, they commit themselves to Jesus the Messiah, and God's Spirit dwells within them. They have God's power through His Holy Spirit, which shields them from the Devil and his demons. Believers cannot be destroyed unless they destroy themselves through sin.

If they manage to destroy themselves, the consequences will wipe out humanity without the Devil needing to lift a finger. And if humanity ceases to exist, God's creation will die.

As worldwide conflict among people intensified, Satan hoped that God would send His angels who guard the gates of hell to help stop humanity from destroying itself. That would create a vulnerability in hell's defenses.

Satan plans to assault and tear down the gates of hell to free his worst angels. He believes this would shift the balance of power between himself and God. With that new power, Satan thinks he could finally seize God's throne and exile Him from heaven.

"But he will fail! He will fail!" Michael exclaimed.

"Satan doesn't realize that 'greater is He that is in you than he that is in the world.'" That's why God sent His Son to be the Savior of everyone. You are also His son and daughter. You have more power than angels because the Holy Spirit's power lives in you through faith. You will defeat Satan. You have found grace in the Lord's eyes. Lucifer can't win until all of God's army is dead—that includes both of you.

"How can all this be?" Bert asked incredulously.

The battle with Satan will unfold here, in your home. You and Susan are humanity's last hope. You are the only ones left alive. God placed you in this house nestled among these mountains to protect you from the destructive effects of humanity's atomic war.

"Like Moses in the cleft of the rock for protection," Susan responded.

Michael smiled.

While we battle Satan underground to maintain control of hell, you will stay in this cellar. You can come out each day and eat from the Tree of Life in your yard. If you go off your property, Satan will catch you, and everything will be lost. He can't force you to do anything, only lead you into temptation. The Devil wants you to reject Christ through sin and die. Remember, he is a liar.

Do you understand my instructions?

Bert and Susan nodded. Bert's expression indicated he believed.

Michael disappeared.

***

Bert and Susan stayed in the cellar, but this time a light followed them, as if it came from their bodies. They couldn't see any light coming from themselves, which confused them, but they decided that God must be causing it. Whatever the reason, they liked it.

I'm hungry, Bert.

Okay, let's eat from the tree that Michael told us about.

For the second time, they left the house and saw something horrifying. The wind, fire, and radiation had caused destruction everywhere, turning the entire landscape into a scorched hellscape. A few skeletons of neighboring houses remained, blackened and smoldering. The couple also found a handful of steel-and-brick buildings still standing, their windows blown out and interiors engulfed in flames.

The blast vaporized most of the wooden structures, leaving nothing inside but human skeletons with a few pieces of clothing still attached to their bones. Bert and Susan saw no other living people. Burning cars and trucks had become hollow shells. Animal skeletons were scattered around. They saw and heard no birds.

So many trees had been uprooted, their blackened branches reaching aimlessly toward the dull yellow sky that blocked the sun.

"Help me, please!" a hoarse, gravelly voice called out.

Bert and Susan saw someone trying to crawl out from beneath a section of the metal roof. The man stood, weakly supporting himself on the fender of a burned-out car. His torn and scorched clothes revealed burned arms. The fire had scorched the hair on his head down to the scalp.

The man staggered toward Bert and Susan, wheezing as he tried to breathe.

"Water ... water ... I need water." He groaned and collapsed to the ground. Susan ran into the house and grabbed a cup of water. Bert knelt beside him and helped the man sit up so he could drink.

"Please help my wife," he begged weakly. "She is alive under the fallen roof but can't speak or walk."

On impulse, Bert ran toward the fallen roof to rescue the stranger's wife. Susan shouted at him to stop just inches before her husband left their property.

Just then, Bert heard a woman's voice, though it was barely audible. "Help!" she gasped.

"You can't, Bert!" Susan shrieked. "Remember what Michael said: 'Leave the property, and Satan will capture you.'"

Bert's eyes widened with recognition. He stepped back toward the strange man, pointed at him, and told him to go. "You are a liar and a fraud."

The stranger glared at him before transforming into a slimy snake, hissing and slithering away.

***

Susan and Bert picked fruits from the Tree of Life in their yard and felt amazed. The tree bore every kind of fruit and nut known to man. All kinds of vegetables grew around the tree's roots. They ate and ate until they couldn't eat any more.

Returning to the cellar, they prayed together, thanking the Lord for the food and protection from the Devil. They fell asleep peacefully and contentedly.

Hours later, Bert awoke to sharp pain and cramping in his stomach. His stomach rebelled; he swallowed hard to stop himself from vomiting. He tried to stand so he could go outside, but dizziness prevented him from climbing the ladder.

He called Susan for help, but she didn't answer. Frightened by the silence, Bert turned and knelt beside her, calling her name several times.

"Susan! Babe, please wake up!" No answer. Bert shook her. Still no response. Panic took over.

He called for help, but no one responded. He crawled toward the ladder, then grabbed it to stand and support himself.

Lord, please help me!

Carefully climbing each ladder rung, Bert made his way to the kitchen floor. The pain in his stomach was so severe that he fainted for a moment. When he regained consciousness, he managed to crawl into the yard. He lay face up, praying to God not to let Susan die.

A white angel hovered overhead and asked if he had eaten from the Tree of Life.

Yes.

I'm sorry to hear that. God sent me to tell you that someone lied to you. Because you and your wife ate from the tree, you both will die. Do you understand that this battle is about gaining control of hell? Well, I won. Michael lied to you. Now, curse God and die.

"What is your name?" Bert asked with suspicion.

I am Satan, the true archangel, and I am finally the god of this miserable planet.

I won't die. You're lying.

Bert's pain began to fade as he stood up to face Satan. As he looked into the Devil's black eyes, thunder and lightning started to roar from the sky. Lightning bolts struck all around the Devil, making him tremble and hide his face.

The yellow clouds dispersed, and the sun shone brightly once more. Thousands of angels appeared, encircling Satan and Bert. Trumpets began to sound, and the angels parted ways as the Red Sea had parted thousands of years ago. This time, it wasn't the people of Israel walking on dry land; a single person on a white horse slowly approached through the space between the angels.

The rider dismounted, paused, and approached Bert and Satan. His eyes blazed like fire. He wore a crown with a name no one knew. Blood stained his white vestment. Across his vestment and thighs, the words 'KING OF KINGS AND LORD OF LORDS' burned in blood-red letters.

Bert kneeled before the King. Satan remained standing but turned his back and covered his face.

Bert, stand up! Our Father in heaven is proud to call you and Susan His son and daughter. Because of your faith and acts of obedience, you and Susan have defeated Satan. Your actions have turned the tide in the war against Hell.

Check behind you.

Bert spun around. Susan was alive! She hurried over and hugged him.

Our Father has answered your prayer, and I will return later to take you to heaven. As for this miserable creature, Satan will no longer bother you.

The King of Kings transformed Satan into a snake, grabbed him by his tail, and threw him away.

In an instant, God hurled Bert and Susan back into their cellar.

They paused, momentarily stunned.

What just happened, Bert?

Who knows? But look! The cellar is finished, and even the staircase to the kitchen is complete.

When they stepped outside, something caught them off guard.

"The atomic bombs didn't change anything; everything remained the same," Bert exclaimed. "The houses and people are back, and the birds are singing again. How can this be? And what did the King of Kings mean when He granted our prayer?"

Susan smiled knowingly. "God restored His creation, and Jesus is the King of Kings."

Okay, but which prayer did He answer?

That was for me, Bert. You're going to become a father.

9

Chapter 9

"SEARCHING HEAVEN FOR YOU"

"Allen, check the car brakes before we leave to go over the mountain to our vacation cabin at the lake," said Beth.

"They're fine. Don't worry."

Allen had spent the family's budget money on the cabin at the lake. He didn't want Beth to know. She and the children deserved to have a vacation. Besides, God would take care of them.

The mountain pass road, icy and dangerous, disappeared into a thick fog bank. Snow started to fall, reducing visibility to almost nothing—just white and black. Beth shivered as the cold seeped into her bones. From the back seat, the children's whines broke the silence.

"Children, please stop whining. Focus on your homework for school. You don't want to spend your vacation doing homework, do you?" Her knuckles, bone-white, pressed against the steering wheel, her hands gripping the plastic so tightly that her fingers ached.

As she entered Dead Man's Curve at the mountain's summit, a huge truck sped toward her in her lane. She jerked the wheel right, missed the truck, and slammed the car into the mountainside.

The truck roared past as Beth's car ricocheted across the pavement into the oncoming lane. She slammed on the brakes, the pedal sinking uselessly to the floor. The vehicle flipped over the guardrail, landed on its side, then rolled and tumbled, shattering until the boulders at the bottom of the ravine stopped it.

The crash triggered a landslide; within seconds, tons of rocks, dirt, and snow slid down, burying the car and forming a hidden tomb.

Beth whispered her final dying words to Allen, but no one heard them.

Brother Allen slumped at his office desk, surrounded by heavy silence. Today marked the thirtieth anniversary of his wife, son, and daughter's disappearance. The law enforcement report stated, "We found no trace of them." No evidence remained to investigate. "Case closed."

For thirty years, Allen convinced himself he couldn't recall his wife's last words on that tragic day. Even now, just before leaving to preach a revival a hundred miles away, the memory still slips from him.

Time haunted him. Did her words hold the key? Was he responsible for their death? He was too afraid to admit he truly understood her words. His guilt stayed with him every day.

He carried guilt like an anchor around his neck. The weight drained him both physically and mentally.

***

The cabin air was heavy with the smell of pine and excitement. Beth was thrilled about a family weekend, a surprise for their son's birthday. Horses awaited the children; the trails beckoned.

The car vanished—one moment it was on the road; the next, it was gone. After the snow melted and the highway was cleared, search teams found no wreckage, no tracks slipping off the mountainside. The landslide had erased any sign that the car had left the road. The family and any evidence of an accident were buried beneath dirt and rocks. Only an unsettling silence remained, and a theory that seemed like a cruel joke.

As a last resort, law enforcement questioned Allen about his family's disappearance. They knew he had a solid alibi, but they focused only on him, which proved ineffective.

Police agencies believed his wife and two children had disappeared and were dead. Were they murdered? Did his family leave him for a different life? Did

God take them somewhere? Allen never lost hope of reuniting with his family.

One last reckless idea lingered—a final, desperate attempt to regain control. If they were dead, perhaps God had the answer. He longed for a chance to search Heaven, find them, and finally end his mental torment.

At least he would know they were dead and in Heaven, and he could accept it. But the troubling question always lingers in his mind: did he cause the family's downfall?

His reason for searching Heaven seemed personal and selfish—like the work of a lunatic.

God allowed the apostle Paul to see Heaven; maybe He would permit Allen to search for his family. Allen qualified as a disciple, didn't he? Searching would confirm their arrival and end this mental torment. God let Paul look. Why not me?

Paul wrote that he went to "the third heaven, paradise," where God resides. What he saw was beyond human understanding, and believers and scholars have long debated his experience. Why would revealing Allen's vision be more controversial?

In Allen's view, Paul's writings accurately describe a journey to "the third heaven, paradise," a place beyond human understanding, and people have debated that claim for centuries. Would revealing Allen's vision be more controversial? Paul spoke of visions he saw, things God forbade him to share. Why? The mystery fueled Allen's hope and his need for more knowledge.

His inability to remember his wife's last words pierced him deeply, like a knife in his gut. Tears streamed down his face. If searching Heaven could reveal the answer to their disappearance, he couldn't share it with anyone. It would remain his and God's secret. Allen started to voice his arguments in sincere prayer.

On one hand, he desperately wants the truth. On the other hand, he's terrified that the truth will condemn him.

***

Exhausted from avoiding the truth by praying for others' pain and sorrows, visiting the sick, writing letters to bereaved families, and preparing sermons for Sunday, he found that none of it helped. He was worn out from running from the truth.

The city streets blurred around him, with bumper-to-bumper traffic and each horn blast just a distant buzz. Allen didn't see the other cars.

A beautiful rainbow shimmered between two buildings—magenta, yellow, and green against the blue sky—God's mercy to Noah. Jesus on the cross, displaying love for humanity through shed blood.

Allen prayed, "Lord, I'd rather know the truth and suffer than live in darkness. Let me search heaven for my family, or take me home."

And then it happened.

The red light at the busy intersection was just a blur of color. He never heard the other car's screeching tires. The screaming, shattering glass, crunching metal, and pleas for help from the accident victims didn't bother him.

Bright lights shone into his eyes. A stiff gurney pressed against his back. A woman's voice cut through the fog: "Doctor, he's waking up."

"Administer three additional cc of propofol."

Darkness surrounded him: no vision, no noise, no pain.

Doctor, his heart has stopped.

The doctor's stethoscope pressed against his chest. He shook his head. "Mark it at 6:02 P.M. as the time of death."

***

Allen's eyes snapped open. White. Just white. A voice cut through the silence. "What manner of thing has the crystal river of Heaven delivered to the shore?"

Two men stood there, dressed in white. One turned to the other and said, "Mark, tell Jesus we have a second visitor."

Alright, Matthew.

"Where am I?" Allen's throat felt dry. "And who are you?"

"I'm Matthew, the author of the Gospel that appears in your printed scrolls. People knew me as the tax collector; others called me Levi."

"*How can you be Matthew?*"Allen rubbed his hands together, a familiar anxiety rising. He's *been dead for centuries.* If this were real, he would be in Heaven.

"Where do you think you are?" Matthew's sharp gaze fixed on him.

I prayed to God in the name of Jesus, asking to come here and search for my family. They had been missing for thirty years, and even the police couldn't find them. The thought twisted my gut. *I love them so much, and their disappearance has driven me crazy.*

"Oh my!" Matthew shook his head. "I don't believe your explanation is completely truthful. Be careful what you ask for; think about the consequences."

I'm telling the truth!

Let's say you're a little mischievous...

What?

Allen, are you here to find your family or to comfort yourself about whether you caused their disappearance?

Allen sighed and shook his head. "Both." The unknown haunted him— that last conversation with his wife before she vanished, words lost in the fog of his memory.

"Very well, Allen," Matthew said. Soon, you'll know the truth. He paused, then said, "Of all people, you should know confessing sins is good for you. Lying does no good in Heaven. Proceed along the crystal river. Moses is waiting for you."

***

The river captivated Allen. He couldn't look away. The channel narrowed, and the current quickened—water shimmered like glass. He reached into the water. A slimy substance slipped past his fingers. The surface was still, with no waves or ripples, but below, the water flowed swiftly. How could it move so fast without creating any waves or ripples? What he saw before him made the river seem insignificant.

Moses stood on the other side of the crystal river, staff raised high. A chasm split the water apart.

Come on over! See? Dry land, right? Talk with me.

Allen couldn't believe what he saw. He stepped onto dry land like the Israelites. The water stopped, forming a wall taller than two men stacked shoulder to shoulder. The water wall and the dry riverbed scene amazed him so much that excitement nearly made him faint.

Moses lowered his staff, and the waters eased back into a gentle flow. "Sit down—that flat rock. Let's talk." You told Matthew you only searched for closure about your family's disappearance, to remember what your wife said before they vanished. Is that your only purpose?

Yes.

If you realize you caused their fate, will you accept that truth?

Yes, I think so.

"Let me explain something, Allen," Moses paused. I never lied to God, but I didn't always follow His instructions. God punished me. I struck a rock for water when I should have spoken to it. People believed my power caused the water to flow.

I took God's glory from Him; He wouldn't let me enter the Promised Land. I died soon after. You don't want to challenge God's judgment or His reasons. You already know: Don't challenge God.

I held onto my faith until Jesus came and preached salvation to me in Sheol. Then I understood. Faith through grace in Jesus Christ—that leads to salvation. He took away my sins and lifted my burden. Always be honest in Heaven. Be truthful with yourself.

Moses's eyebrows knit tightly. "You told law enforcement you had no idea why your family disappeared?"

"I didn't kill my family!"

Then why feel guilty about their disappearance?

Allen's head drooped, chin brushing his chest. A heavy guilt weighed on his stomach. "My wife said something that morning. What was it? The forgotten memory haunted him."

Remember, Allen, confession is good for the soul. Discover the truth about your family. Jesus waits to help.

Allen cast him a curious look.

Now, for you, Heaven has twelve entrance gates. You enter through gate number twelve. Heaven is twelve stories high, and you go to the twelfth floor. We call it the Gentiles floor, and the apostle Paul will meet you at the door. He will guide you to the viewing window, which is as clear as glass, but God will not allow you to interact with those on the other side. They cannot see you. You can only see and hear them.

When you find your answer, you will return to your earthly body and decide what to do with what you saw and heard. I advise you to accept your answer to your question and, in Jesus' name, thank him for answering your prayer. Proceed now. Follow the crystal river; an angel waits for you.

Alright, I will.

***

The river babbled past as Allen strolled along the bank, talking to himself and to God. "Lord, Matthew and Moses seem to think I killed my family, and you know I didn't." His stomach clenched. "Please answer my question—is my family here?"

An angel met Allen along the Crystal River and pointed him toward Heaven's Gate. Allen couldn't believe what he saw. He entered the door labeled number twelve. Instantly, Allen stood before the Apostle Paul.

Paul looked into his eyes and said, "Follow me."

Allen's mind raced as he tried to understand the wonder. I never realized the twelve colors of Heaven's foundations were separate layers. And the beauty of the gold street, the pearl gates, the glowing, brilliant light—I'm at a loss for words.

Paul smiled. "We all were when we first arrived. Here we are at the viewing window. I will leave you now. You can't interact with your family; that would taint heaven with your sin. Moses already gave you instructions. After you receive your answer, you will return to your earthly life."

Allen's gaze was fixed on the empty wall. "Wait! There is nothing here."

Paul said, "After I leave, you will see."

The wall displayed a picture of his family, stunning Allen. He reached out, his fingers pressing against the solid barrier. He felt the cold glass. Thirty years earlier, the fatal accident replayed—he saw, he heard everything, trapped on the other side. His breath hitched.

The white line on the road was barely visible in the rainstorm. Fear tightened in Beth's stomach—this mountain road was treacherous, dangerous, winding.

A sign appeared through the spray: "CAUTION, DEAD MAN'S CURVE." Her breath caught.

Headlights burst around the bend, coming too fast and too close. An 18-wheeler took the curve too sharply, crossed the center line, and headed straight for them. Directly at Beth. Directly at the children.

A scream tore from her throat as she jerked the wheel, her face set in stoic determination. The truck rushed past, a blur of metal and rain. The car scraped against the rocks, a shriek of tearing metal. A jagged edge of rock caught the side panel. The vehicle spun out of control, swerving across the highway toward the mountain's edge.

She slammed on the brakes. The car skidded sideways on the slick pavement, hit the guardrail, and flipped over. Tumbling. Rolling. Over and over.

Impact. Blackness.

The vehicle collided with two large boulders. A wave of rocks followed, breaking the roof apart and covering the car in dirt and stone. Darkness completely engulfed the car.

Allen couldn't breathe. The twisted steel tomb trapped him inside as he watched the last breaths leave his daughter's body.

His son lay on the back seat floor, pinned there but still reaching between the bucket seats, his small fingers grabbing Beth's arm.

A muffled moan through the dust: "Why, Allen, didn't you check the brakes as I asked you?"

Allen's knees buckled as he collapsed onto the cold floor of the viewing room, grief tearing through him like a raw scream. Those words—the ones he had buried for years—confirmed his guilt. He had caused their deaths.

He managed a mumble: "Forgive me, Lord. I remember. I tried to deny it, lied that I couldn't remember. But I knew."

Grief overwhelmed Allen. His chest felt tight, each breath like a sharp blade. Then, a faint sound pierced his pain: Beth's voice, praying inside the wrecked car.

He stopped crying. His eyes stayed fixed on the view screen, but the scene blurred and faded, shifting like static.

A different scene filled his mind—or was it a memory? A picnic spread on sacred ground. Heaven shone around their relatives, bathing them in light. Beth's voice rose in thanks for the meal and God's blessing. *"Please, help Allen not worry. We're safe. We'll wait for him." The* words wrapped around him like a soft, warm blanket.

Then, a sudden, sharp sound: "Doctor, we have a heartbeat."

"It can't be!"

Bright, harsh light seared his eyes. People came into focus, standing over him—a gurney.

His lips moved, the words a gentle whisper: "Thank you, Jesus, for giving me peace and for providing my family with a heavenly home."

He looked up at the faces around him and said, "There's a ravine off Dead Man's Curve. The car's under some rocks—that's where they are. Please send a search team."

10

Chapter 10

"WHAT GOD DOES BEST"

Dressed in green bib overalls, a wide-brimmed straw hat, and a checkered red shirt, Farmer John sat down on a hay bale and sighed.

What other options do I have? "I've done all I know to do to help my wife." He stared at the ground, tracing patterns in the dirt with the toe of his boot. Holding his two-gallon bucket of fowl feed in his lap, frustrated, he dumped the feed out so the barnyard fowls could eat.

Mrs. Leghorn Chicken arrived with her huddling biddies; Mrs. Mallard Duck marched in line with her brood; Mrs. Mama Goose flapped her wings with her goslings; and the barnyard owl clung to her back, her owlets clutching her feathers. They all pecked at and picked up the feed on the ground. The noise of feeding and animal chatter signaled a happy flock of birds.

Usually, Farmer John spoke in his cheerful, bubbly manner and whistled while the chickens ate. But today, he sat quietly with a sad frown. The adult birds noticed his disappointment. They moved closer to Farmer John's boots and pecked at his toe, friendly.

Usually, a big smile would cross his face, and he would say, "Girls, by now I expect you to know the difference between a boot and fowl feed." He'd wink at them, sharing a familiar, private joke. He would never yell or kick them away for pecking his boot.

When Farmer John covered his face with his hands and began to cry, all the barnyard fowl took notice. The barnyard fowl had never seen Farmer John cry or appear so sad. It upset the adult fowls, and they gathered around.

Mrs. Leghorn flapped her wings in distress, making a sound like a tiny storm. "Girls, what in the world is wrong with Farmer John?"

Mrs. Mallard said, "The duck shifted from one webbed foot to the other. "I have never seen a human cry."

"I haven't either," said Mama Goose.

Mrs. Owl said, ruffling her feathers and blinking her large yellow eyes, "I have seen Farmer John's wife, Mary, cry."

"When? When? When?" the other hens asked.

Mrs. Owl balanced herself on the fence post, her yellow eyes locked on the farmhouse.

"Do you girls remember when that big truck ran over Lady Peacock and her family of peppers a few years ago? She came to the crash site and scooped up Lady Peacock and her three little peeps in her arms. She hugged them so tightly that tears streamed down Mary's face. I must admit, girls, my heart ached at the sight of Mary's sadness. I'll never forget, and we hoot owls don't forget." She fluffed her feathers, a hooting sound catching in her throat.

Gosh, girls, what can we do? If Farmer John knew we could hear and understand him, and he could hear us, maybe we could help him, Mrs. Owl hooted.

The hens looked at Farmer John as he cried, feeling so helpless. Mrs. Leghorn remembered all the years Farmer John had spent feeding and caring for the barnyard animals, not just the fowls; he never complained.

She pecked at a nearby seed, then looked up at him with a worried tilt of her head. He would take them to a doctor if they got sick. He would feed them when storms hammered the barnyard with rain. He prepared a safe place for them to eat. Farmer John would fend off attackers, even when buzzards came to steal a meal from their young.

Without thinking of the consequences, Mrs. Leghorn suddenly jumped onto Farmer John's lap. Her claws scraped his denim pants, surprising him. He gently stroked her feathers, slowly running his hand down her back. A tear rolled down his weathered cheek as he moved his hand, and a small, sad smile appeared on his lips.

He smiled and said, "How I wish I could talk to you and you to me. You have never flown to me before, and certainly not let me stroke your feathers. I wonder if you sense my sadness. Thank you for being a friend. God is good to you and me."

Farmer John gently set her back on the ground as her chicks gathered around her. He smiled and headed back to the farmhouse. He wiped his face with a dusty handkerchief, his shoulders slightly drooping.

Mrs. Owl suggested they call Head Hog for a meeting with the fowls; he was the leader of the barnyard and would know what to do. "He is respected among the animals for his wisdom." All the fowl clucked, quacked, and honked at Mrs. Owl's suggestion.

***

His round belly swayed from side to side with each careful step. Moving slowly with tiny strides, the jowl-sagging, fat-nosed, piggy-eared Chester White Head Hog trudged toward the hens waiting there.

"What demands that I leave my cool wallowing hole?" Head Hog grunted, shifting his great weight and squinting at the hens.

The girls burst into lively chatter. The loud noise throughout the barnyard caused a thirty-second pause in all activity. From the fowls' loud commotion, the animals guessed that Head Hog had insulted them. That wouldn't have been unusual for Head Hog; he usually got his way in the barnyard. He was the oldest of all the animals.

Each hen vividly recounted her experiences with Farmer John.

"We are upset," Mrs. Leghorn fluffed her neck feathers as she paced anxiously. "Farmer John is sad."

"When he cried, if we knew how to cry, we would have cried." Mama Goose honked mournfully, stretching her long neck toward the sky.

"We understand what hurt is and how we grieve over tragedy, but this water dropping from the eyes, what kind of reaction is that?" Mrs. Mallard asked. "My ducklings are quacking in sorrow for Farmer John." Mrs. Mallard nodded to a group of sad-sounding ducklings huddled near a puddle.

The owl said, "Farmer John told us he wished we could talk to him and he to us."

Head Hog grunted, stepped back, and scratched his back on the fence post where Mrs. Owl sat. Mrs. Owl screeched and fell off the top of the post, but she landed on Head Hog's head.

Mama Goose said, "What will you do about this, Head Hog? You're the boss." Mama Goose fixed him with a commanding look, her posture challenging.

Head Hog said, "This is serious!" Head Hog stomped a cloven hoof, his piggy ears twitching with genuine concern. "I have never known Farmer John not to smile when he's with the barnyard animals. Why, I've heard him talk to us as if we were his children, and I've heard him sing. I hope he isn't sick. We will meet tonight in the barn for a meeting." Head Hog's snout twitched, emphasizing the point. "Please ask everyone to be very quiet when arriving at the barn. We don't want to wake Farmer John."

***

Head Hog grunted and snorted as two pigs pushed and lifted his large, round backside onto Farmer John's big red toolbox. Head Hog wobbled from side to side and called the meeting to order.

"My friends." Head Hog wiped a hoof across his brow. We face a problem we've never encountered before. You heard the gossip the hens spread today about Farmer John. We don't know what Farmer John's troubles are.

If he doesn't tell us what's wrong, we won't know what's wrong with him or how to help him. If his issue is life-threatening, it could put our lives at risk," he paced in a small circle on the toolbox, which wobbled dangerously.

If Farmer John isn't here to take care of us, I'd rather not think about it. Please suggest some solutions.

"I have one." Mrs. Leghorn Hen flapped her wings, nearly losing her balance on the crowded floor. "Farmer John told me, and the other hens heard him say it. He wished he could talk with us, and we wished we could talk with him. Does anyone know how to do this?"

A visiting eagle spoke, telling the barnyard animals that an eagle had talked to people in the Book of Revelation, warning them from their Creator.

"Who told you that, eagle?" Mama Goose leaned her long neck forward, narrowing one eye suspiciously.

While resting on a church steeple, I heard a man read a story from the Bible. It was a judgment from our Creator on the people of the earth. The eagle flew, warning the people to beware. Our Creator made a special bond between animals and humans.

"I have never heard such a tale." The mouse flicked his tail nervously.

"Has anyone else ever heard of such miraculous communication?" said Head Hog. He swiveled his large ears toward the captivated audience. There was silence. A fly buzzed near a dusty windowpane; otherwise, the barn was quiet.

Then, a voice from a dark stall said, "I have." All eyes turned toward the sound, a collective twitching of tails and ears.

Head Hog's curly tail twitched as if lightning had struck him.

He dug his hooves in and said, "Come out of the dark and tell us about it."

A tiny, droopy-eared donkey with a smile ambled out of the darkness and stood before Head Hog.

"Stop grinning and tell us your story." Head Hog snorted, kicking up a small puff of straw.

Our ancestors told a story passed down through generations about a man hitting his donkey. While he was riding her, she saw an angel on the highway with a sword drawn, ready to kill her owner. The donkey refused to go down the road to protect her master. Her master beat her for it.

The donkey gently lowered his head, a shadow passing over his eyes. God has granted us special powers to see him. Humans can only dream of such a gift.

God allowed the donkey to speak to her master about what she saw on the road. She explained that she had tried to protect her master by avoiding that road.

The animals gasped.

Head Hog snorted, pawing impatiently at the ground. "What happened to the donkey's owner?"

"I don't know," the donkey said with a shrug.

Now listen. I think we're onto something. Head Hog looked around the barn, making eye contact with the others. "Do we not know the story of Noah and the ark? Did not God speak to our ancestors, telling them to board the ark? Did not some sacrifice their lives so that Noah and his family could survive? God gave us a special relationship with people." He nodded once, decisively.

We share a special bond with God, and I believe none of us in this barn tonight should go to sleep. We should pray for God to give us the ability to communicate with Farmer John. We need to understand his problem. Farmer John has cared for us, and now it's our turn to care for him.

Nobody leaves this barn tonight. We will pray to God the Creator for a solution in His Son's name, Jesus.

The barnyard animals had no idea that Farmer John was praying to God, who made both humans and animals.

***

The next day, Mr. Rooster flew to the top of the barn and crowed his wake-up call to both the animals and humans. Half-asleep and exhausted, the animals slowly shuffled out of the barn. Soon after, they heard Farmer John's screen door slam shut as he headed to feed them.

The barnyard animals slowly and carefully gathered around Farmer John as he sat on his hay bale, holding a feed bucket for the fowl. He looked down at his worn boots, avoiding their eyes. He said, "I don't know what else to do." He kept a straight face and scattered a little feed on the ground, then noticed the animals gathering around him.

Farmer John pointed to the animals gathered around and said, "My friends, we share a bond. I often sit here and tell you about the world's events and my family. You are my best friends."

After praying until early this morning, he took a deep, shaky breath and wiped his eyes with a calloused hand. "I wanted to share my troubles with you. I know you are animals, and you can't help me solve my human problems. However, after praying to God for help, a strange urge overcame me to tell my friends my troubles."

Mrs. Leghorn Chicken flew over and landed beside Farmer John on the hay bale. Farmer John smiled at Mrs. Leghorn Chicken.

"I know all of you don't understand what I am saying, but all the animals are here in the barnyard this morning looking at me. If I didn't know better, I would think you could hear and understand me. Farmer John chuckled sadly, running a hand through his gray hair. Nonsense, but talking with you makes me feel better, so here is my trouble." The animals stepped closer to Farmer John.

"My wife Mary has a disease called cancer, and it's deadly. If she doesn't get an operation to remove it..." He chuckled sadly, running a hand through his gray hair. The animals looked at one another because they sometimes had the same disease.

I don't have enough money to cover her surgery. We've been married for fifty-one years, and I love her. I prayed and prayed, but nothing has changed.

I tried to borrow money from the bank, but they refused to lend more because the farm was already heavily mortgaged. He suddenly stood up, pacing the small space in front of the hay bale. "I don't know what I'll do if she dies!" Farmer John hid his face again as he cried. The animals trudged back to the barn.

With the help of two pigs, Head Hog reached the top of the toolbox. He cleared his throat loudly to get their attention.

Okay, any thoughts?

"Mr. Rat and I do." Weasel jabbed his thumb at his partner.

Head Hog shouted, "Tell us!" and stepped forward, his eyes shining with anticipation.

Mr. Weasel and Mr. Rat stepped to the front of the animals, acting like two escaped convicts; they moved their heads side to side, their eyes darting as they waited for someone to catch them.

Rat and I have spent our lives stealing paper from banks and businesses. It bears the words "In God We Trust," along with numbers. I believe that's what Farmer John calls money. If so, we have bags and bags of it.

Mr. Rat said, "We take it because it's fun to annoy humans, and we make nests out of it. Weasel and I will gladly give it to Farmer John to help his wife."

"How can we trust you?" Head Hog asked.

"Because we won't lie to you." Mr. Rat placed a paw over his heart sincerely. "Do you think we act like rats?" All the animals laughed in the barn.

That night, the army ants marched into the barn and stood at attention while Horse heaved the bags of money onto their backs. They carried the ten large garbage bags full of cash to the porch door that Farmer John usually used to access the barnyard.

The next day, after Mr. Rooster announced the morning wake-up, the animals gathered by the barnyard fence to watch Farmer John come out and find the bags of money.

As usual, Farmer John stepped out of the porch door. He stumbled back, falling into the bags. One burst open, spilling green paper all over him. He got up, wiping his eyes with a muddy hand. "For God's sake, what are these bags of—Praise God! Praise God!" Water streamed from his eyes as he walked to the fence where the barnyard animals stood in a line, smiling in their own way. Farmer John stopped, wiped his eyes, and looked at the animals.

He said, "You understand me. You animals always know how to listen, and I wish you could tell me you do. I can't imagine how you barnyard animals did this, but through the same God who created us all, I know you had a hand in it. I thank God and all the animals, and I love you all."

Mrs. Leghorn Chicken rushed over to Farmer John and pecked at his boot.

11

Chapter 11

"SEED SOWER"

Jessie McGottor, the butcher, asked Jesus to forgive him and save him. With a sorrowful and repentant heart, Jessie turned his repentance into a burning desire to share the message of Christ the Savior with others.

But where or how should he start?

He trusted his pastor, but the pastor's responsibilities limited his ability to train or advise Jessie in effective witnessing personally. Jessie wrung his hands, showing his anxiety about not having enough guidance. He worried he wouldn't be able to answer questions about how, where, and when to witness.

He was at a loss for words to express empathy for others' misfortune. He couldn't shed tears at every bad event people faced. Emotional responses were absent from his nature.

Although he had cried when he experienced salvation, did that mean everyone reacted the same way? But that wasn't the same as empathy.

Jessie immersed himself in every pamphlet, handout, and tract about salvation and witnessing for Jesus Christ. He felt prepared. Moreover, a book he read in the library suggested that the best way to learn personal witnessing was through individual experience. The question was where to start.

Jessie remembered the words of Isaiah the prophet in the Bible: 'Whom shall I send, and who will go for us?' Then I said, 'Here am I; send me.' He slammed his fist down on the heavy wooden cutting block, the sound dull and final.

Jessie hung up his butcher's apron for the day. He had worked as a butcher at his neighborhood grocery store for twenty years and knew almost everyone in the community. He thought about all the people he was familiar with—surely someone needed help. He decided to start with his meat customers. Tomorrow would be a good day to begin sharing his faith in Jesus.

Driving home from work, Jessie stopped at his favorite poolroom for a couple of beers with his friends. He held the steering wheel so tightly that his knuckles turned white. They would listen to him give his testimony about Jesus Christ. Many of his poolroom buddies had been schoolmates, and most of them had cheered him at his wedding. They would listen to him.

The pool hall was lively, with many bubbas relaxing after a tough day's work. His buddies monopolized the second table. Patrons filled every stool at the bar except for one — Jessie's usual spot at the end of the row.

"Hey, Jessie!" Joseph waved his hand to get his friend's attention. "Bring your beer over here and play nine-ball with us."

"I'll be right there." He ordered two longnecks and set them on the courtesy table by the wall. Then he grabbed his cue stick from the house rack on the wall.

Are we playing for our usual quarter per ball?

Yeah.

Who's breaking?

You are.

Jessie smashed the cue ball into the nine-ball formation, scattering them across the table. Not sinking a ball into any of the six pockets, Jessie stepped aside for the next player while retrieving his New Testament from his back pocket.

Fellows, I don't know if you heard, but I was saved last Sunday at church.

"What did you say?" Tom asked. "You got saved? Were you drowning?"

Sure! I was drowning in sin, so I asked Jesus to save me. Jessie looked directly at Tom, his expression sincere and unwavering.

Howie said, "Do tell us what that means."

Jessie drank about half of his beer—a subconscious way to calm his nerves.

He inhaled deeply.

After listening to the preacher, I realized I had sinned against God. God sent Jesus, his Son, to die for me and cover my sins. Jesus paid that debt by suffering death on the cross.

The preacher warned me that unless I accepted Jesus's gift of atonement, I would face eternal hellfire for my lies, cheating, and sins. To avoid that fate, I asked Jesus for forgiveness in His name and admitted I was a sinner. I welcomed Jesus into my life and received forgiveness freely. The beer felt cold in his hand, and he took a long sip.

Riley said, "For God's sake, Jessie, every weekend when my wife comes back from a business trip, I have to say all that to her. It's no big deal."

They all started laughing.

Jessie ordered two more beers and drank them. He slammed the empty glasses onto the sticky counter. He felt calmer now, although something told him he'd have to stop doing this someday.

Someone suggested increasing the wager to one dollar per ball and ten dollars for the nine-ball.

"Wait until you hear about the virgin birth," said Jessie after wiping his mouth and ordering two more beers. Now he was calmer than ever.

For the next thirty minutes, Jessie played the bar's clown, sharing stories about Mary—a virgin—being pregnant and about the baby growing into Jesus, who eventually rose from the dead. Meanwhile, he was losing money on billiard bets. He became so relaxed that he bought a round of beers for everyone in the bar. Jessie had to cash his paycheck to cover his gambling losses and all the beers he'd bought.

He was now so calm yet excited that he announced a contest to everyone in the bar. The person who could tell the best story would get a free beer from him.

He climbed onto a barstool, almost losing his balance, and raised his glass to the room. Jessie himself won the competition when he told the story of Mary impregnated by a ghost. So he rewarded himself with another beer.

Finally, the bartender refused to sell Jessie more beer and asked him to leave.

***

The next morning, Jessie's wife slammed the door when she left the house. She worked as a seamstress at the local garment factory.

Jessie remembered only a few words she had yelled at him before leaving. She said she had no money for groceries or rent. She stared him down and also said she was leaving him.

His head throbbed so intensely with pain that he couldn't remember how he got home or the poolroom experience from the day before. Jessie could remember that he had witnessed for God and hoped it came out of his mouth okay.

Drinking and witnessing didn't go well. The seeds planted were damaged.

He still had unanswered questions about how, when, and where.

Suddenly, he realized he was running late for work. He splashed water on his face, but he still felt foggy.

The manager greeted him when he arrived at the grocery store. Jessie was thirty minutes late for work.

"McGoatter, you're thirty minutes late. What do you have to say about your lateness?"

Sir, my wife wanted to celebrate last night, and I felt a little dizzy when I woke up this morning. We won't celebrate that way anymore.

I hope you didn't! You're wearing a tennis shoe on one foot and a black rubber boot on the other. And Jessie, your fly is down. Get to work.

"Yes, sir!" Jessie zipped up his fly as he stepped behind the meat counter. He muttered under his breath, "My name ain't McGoatter."

His assistant grinned goofily. "Welcome back, boss."

Red-faced, Jessie hurried into the meat locker of the freezer.

Realizing he didn't do very well on his first attempt to witness for Jesus, he came up with another plan to try at the end of the workday. He decided to stop by the local library. The library was a quiet, well-organized place, and he was a member.

At the end of Jessie's shift, the store manager told him to go home, get some rest, and be on time the next day.

***

Jessie pulled into the public library's parking lot—carrying his New Testament and a notepad from the meat department. He was ready to witness for Jesus.

Jessie entered, passing the elderly librarian, who looked over the top of her glasses with a quiet, mannerly "Hello." Her eyeglass lanyard hung down to her cheeks, reminding him of his high school librarian, who wore large, round earrings.

Dust fibers floated in the sunlight streaming through the tall windows. As he walked down the aisles of books, he searched for someone to share God's message of saving grace.

He spotted his first target—a young woman, possibly a college student. She was engrossed in reading a book and didn't notice Jessie.

Ma'am, are you saved?

The young woman was startled. "Saved from what?"

"Hell!" Jessie exclaimed excitedly.

I don't know. I've never given it much thought.

I want to share a few thoughts about God and explain salvation to you.

No, the lady shook her head firmly. "Please, not now. I need to study."

"Okay." Jessie handed her a note with his church's name, address, and phone number. "We'd love to see you at our church on Sunday. And if you have any questions about salvation, please call me."

Jessie moved on to find someone else.

A group of six teenagers sat at a table studying together. Jessie prepared six notes, each with one question: "Are you saved?" followed by "Regardless of your condition, we invite you to our church." He walked around the table, carefully placing a note before each person, then moved on.

A satisfied smile touched his lips. He felt proud of his plan and the actions he had taken. He moved to the magazine rack and looked for sports magazines. Finding one, he sat at a small table near a window to read. Then he noticed a police car parked in front of the library and a policeman walking toward the entrance.

He found an interesting article and didn't notice the policeman now standing at his table.

The officer asked, "Sir, will you please follow me outside the front entrance?" The officer gestured toward the door with an open palm.

Jessie complied with the policeman's request.

Sir, solicitation is not permitted in the library. Please return your magazine to the librarian and exit.

"But, sir, I was not soliciting. I was witnessing for Jesus." Jessie stepped back, his hand rising to his chest.

You asked several people to come to your church, using your grocery store notepad with its letterhead stamped at the top of each note. Do you see that sign beside the entrance? The officer pointed to a small sign that read, "No Soliciting." The officer gently took the magazine from his hand. "Please leave, sir."

Jessie ran a hand through his thinning hair; his smile faded. He no longer felt proud of his actions and disapproved of civil disobedience. But then the parable of the Sower of Seeds came to mind. From that parable, he believed that those in the library lacked any spiritual roots to accept the knowledge of salvation.

***

After praying at home for God's help, he devised a new plan for witnessing the next day. He decided to share his faith with people he knew, beginning with his workplace, since everyone there felt like a friend.

The next day, Jessie arrived at work early and waited for his boss to unlock the grocery store. Then Jessie stood outside the front door and greeted both employees and customers with a cheerful welcome: "Good morning! Jesus loves you." He had handouts prepared on the store's notepad and was happy until the store owner came out, red-faced, and glared at Jessie.

"You can't do this at this store. It's in our employees' policy manual. You've been hungover, late, improperly dressed for work, and now this. That's it. You're fired. Leave now."

Jessie was speechless. His jaw clenched as he stared at the floor, shuffled to his car, got in, and then burst into bitter tears. He slammed the car door shut.

He prayed, "I'm done, Lord. You can scratch me off your list. I am not worthy. I tried." He buried his face in his hands and gripped the steering wheel. He stomped on the gas, the engine roaring as the car lunged forward.

Sad, rejected, humiliated, and scared, he drove through the busy city streets toward home. How was he going to explain losing his job to his wife?

Then a little girl darted into a crosswalk. Jessie slammed on his brakes, but the car in front of him didn't see her.

Bam!

The little girl was thrown high into the air above the car, which moved a short distance before coming to a stop. She lay on the hard asphalt, unresponsive. The accident had severely injured her.

Jessie jumped out of his car and knelt beside the little girl. She did not breathe. He shouted for someone to help. The crowd just stared, took videos on their cell phones, and did nothing. A woman nearby, filming with her phone, let out a nervous laugh.

Jessie nervously performed mouth-to-mouth resuscitation, being careful not to move her neck in case of injury. He placed his ear on her chest, but he heard no heartbeat. Nothing.

He found her breastbone and the right spot to deliver chest compressions. After several minutes of mouth-to-mouth rescue and chest compressions, her breathing still had not started. His shoulders slumped, a tear mixing with the sweat on his forehead.

He raised his hands to heaven and said, "Lord, in the name of Jesus, please let this little girl live. I don't know what else to do."

Jessie kept performing mouth-to-mouth resuscitation until the little girl suddenly took a deep breath and yelled loudly. Jessie flinched back, startled, then quickly leaned in again. She looked at Jessie and hugged him with her only good arm, crying and asking for her mother.

Jessie softly started singing the Lord's Prayer as he remembered it from church. The little girl stopped crying and kept telling Jessie she loved him. A siren blared, and he hoped it was an ambulance. He wiped sweat from his forehead, listening carefully as the siren drew nearer.

What is your name?

"Abby."

The ambulance arrived, and EMTs secured the little girl onto a stretcher to take her away, but she insisted that Jessie come with her. So Jessie held her hand as they headed to the hospital. Abby tightly clung to his fingers, her small hand warm in his. She asked Jessie to sing that song again.

At the hospital, Abby wouldn't let go of his hand until he assured her it was safe to see a doctor. He gently rubbed her knuckles with his thumb, trying to offer reassurance.

He sat in the waiting room, waiting for Abby's parents to arrive and learn about the little girl's condition.

He sat crying, praying, and softly singing the Lord's Prayer. A man and a woman entered the waiting room and asked for Jessie McGottor.

Jessie quickly stood up. "I am Jessie McGottor."

The woman went up to Jessie and slapped him multiple times across the face until her husband pulled her back.

"Lady, I—" Jessie stumbled back, his cheek burning. Jessie broke down in tears, fighting to hold them back. He stepped into the hallway, where the doctor was heading toward the waiting room. He leaned against the cool wall, his chest heaving.

He recognized Jessie as the man who had taken the little girl to the hospital. He reported that she would be fine and praised Jessie for performing CPR so effectively. Jessie nodded, still shaken from the slap and the good news. He still had unanswered questions about how, when, and where.

Jessie returned home, still unemployed, depressed, and worried about his wife and future. Suddenly, the door splintered open, and his wife walked in. He flinched, and his blood pressure spiked in his ears. "Have you heard the news going around town?"

"No."

He rubbed his hand over his face, feeling the three-day stubble scrape against his palm.

Then someone knocked on the open door, and a man and the woman who had slapped Jessie entered. The woman quickly pulled Jessie into a hug. "Sorry, I slapped you. The doctor corrected me, saying the other man caused the accident."

Abby's parents repeated what she and the doctor had told them about Jessie and what he had done to save their child. The mother wiped away a tear from her eye. "We are so grateful for your Christian heroic act."

The little girl's father looked into her eyes. His gaze was sincere and straightforward. "Because of the kind of person you are, we want to be saved."

Jessie replied, a genuine smile spreading across his face—the first in days. "Praise the name of Jesus. Who would have thought?"

Abby's father owned a nationwide chain of grocery stores. He offered Jessie a job and allowed him to witness for Jesus to anyone at any time while working.

***

Abby recovered well, and because of the experience, Jessie became a stronger Christian. However, no one answered Jessie's questions about how, where, and when to witness. He brushed his hair—a nervous habit he hadn't yet broken. Ultimately, Jessie found the answers through his own experiences.

When the pastor quoted these words spoken by Jesus to the apostles, they made more sense than ever: "The Holy Spirit will teach you all things, and you will remember all that I have said to you."

12

Chapter 12

"THE WHITE ROBE"

The door burst open and slammed against the wall as Richard Davenport's family sat around the table enjoying their Sunday lunch.

Grandpa John stormed into the house. "Escape now! You don't have time to waste! A red monster that looks like a giant red lizard has come to Stonewall." His voice cracked, strained with panic. Run!

Grandpa realized he'd missed the rapture, or whatever was supposed to happen. He had followed Christian traditions his whole life, and they had helped him grow. But now he understood that practicing religion alone wasn't enough to follow Jesus as Savior truly. Because he lacked faith, he believed God had condemned him to eternal damnation. Missing this, he felt the antichrist had already come.

Unfortunately, he had taught his family to follow rituals and the law rather than to accept grace through faith. Bobby pressed his palms together, his voice barely a whisper. Now they believed they had missed the rapture and the chance for eternal life. Still, Grandpa couldn't accept that his family would end up in hell.

He would willingly sacrifice his life if Jesus were merciful to his family. However, first, he needed to convince his family, especially his grandchildren, to leave so they could come to know Jesus.

Richard jerked back from the dinner table. "What in tarnation did you say,

Dad?" Who's here? Escape, run from what?

Richard's eyes darted between his father and the window, and a knot formed in his stomach. Fearing his dad would have a heart attack, Richard grabbed a chair for him. He placed a hand on his father's shoulder, had him sit down, and stood beside him.

"Did you say a giant red lizard came to Stonewall, North Carolina?" Richard's hand on his father's shoulder clenched slightly, fingers digging in.

"Yes, I did say that." He wiped a sleeve across his sweaty brow.

Grandpa John, out of breath and red-faced, suspiciously glanced at the windows and door, frequently turning his head as he looked for something.

Richard was worried that his father was developing dementia. He ran his hand through his hair, furrowing his brow with concern. Since losing his wife of fifty years, his father had sometimes shown minor signs of forgetfulness and confusion. But everything changed after that day, when so many people vanished.

Grandpa John continued, "Yes, he appeared out of nowhere. Like, poof! There he stood behind me in the church while I was preaching. A giant lizard with scaly skin and a long red tail was standing on its hind legs inside the sanctuary. A row of sharp spikes ran down its backbone all the way to the front door. He paused, taking another deep, shaky breath, eyes wide."

Its feet had toe claws. The lizard's spiky, snake-like head almost touched the church ceiling. Its short, scaly arms had human hands with sharp fingernails as long as rulers." He paused, taking another deep, shaky breath, eyes wide.

"Children, I tell you, he was a devilish red dragon walking on his hind legs and dragging his tail. He was an awful sight." The rest of the family exchanged glances. Richard gently squeezed his wife's hand beneath the table.

Grandpa pressed on. "The churchwomen screamed. A few men fled, abandoning their families and rushing out the church door. Other people fainted and cried. Families huddled together, holding each other. It was chaos and fear." A distant siren wailed outside, a familiar sound now, causing everyone to jump.

Weeks earlier, the pastor had vanished during what was supposed to be the rapture, an event none of them had taken seriously. If it happened at all, this rapture was so quick that no one saw a thing. Since then, Grandpa John, a lay preacher, has preached every Sunday to the people who remained behind.

He and the church members realized they had missed this event, which they had always dismissed as fantasy. Fear overtook them at the thought of missing it because they doubted and lacked faith in Jesus Christ.

They grew desperate for salvation but believed they could never reach it and thought they had lost all hope. Now, they realized that Satan must have sent an antichrist to them.

Grandpa John continued, "The monster moved like a dragon, and its front claws clicked on the wooden floor. Its sharp, red-spiked tail scraped the ends of the wooden pews and rattled as it walked. I tried to move, to run, but something glued my feet to the floor."

I couldn't believe what I was seeing. A cold shiver ran down my spine, and I couldn't speak or move. The monster shoved me away from the pulpit and said, "Satan sent me to guide the people of Stonewall through the catastrophic fall of world governments. He calls me Assistant and has named me Red Devil."

Scared and flustered, Alice, Richard's wife, placed her napkin on the table, silently prayed, then whispered barely audibly, "Am I lost? And my family? Jesus, please forgive me."

Ten-year-old Bobby noticed his mother's worried face—her bowed head, watering eyes, and trembling hands. He moved to the chair beside her, took her hands, and with his big blue eyes and gentle voice asked, "What happened, Mother?" He softly squeezed her fingers.

She pulled him onto her lap and hugged him as he began to whimper. Tears rolled down her face, blurring the outline of the boy's hair. She didn't know how to answer his question: "I need to ask more questions to understand all that's happened." She gently rocked him, a silent promise conveyed in her motion.

Richard encouraged Alice to speak. With Bobby's adorable baby face staring at her, Alice tugged at the hem of her shirt. "When does our government collapse, and what should we do?"

Grandpa pressed his hand to his forehead, his face strained with worry. "I have no idea. And I suspect similar situations are happening all over the world." But what I know for sure is that when I left the church, the Red Devil tore it apart. I saw him go from house to house, announcing that he controlled everything and that the Christian era was over. He is on his way here." He pointed a trembling finger toward the door. "You must run."

Grandpa John knew he had to sacrifice his life to save his family. He straightened up, facing forward squarely. "I'll run interference to give you all the time to escape. The Red Devil will be distracted by my tall tales."

The family laughed, knowing he could tell them.

"But run where, Dad?" Richard's eyes darted around the room as if looking for an immediate answer.

Grandpa stood and placed his hand on Richard's shoulder, giving it a reassuring squeeze. "Go to my cabin on Sanctuary Mountain. I've equipped the cabin with everything you need. Your grandmother and I lived there for half our lives, and we kept it in good condition. It still has all the modern conveniences. You'll live 2,300 feet up the side of the mountain. Red Devil will not be able to see you, but you will be able to see him."

Grandpa assured his family that each night he would stay in touch by signaling Morse code with his spotlight through the skylight in their Stonewall home. If the signal failed, he would hide a message in the old oak tree at the base of the mountain, where the trail to the hidden cabin begins.

You'll need to walk to the cabin. Red Devil might see the car and destroy it as you leave. A three- or four-hour walk isn't bad. He tugged at his bottom lip, weighing the plan. "If you leave at sundown, you can arrive by midnight with some extra time."

Alice paced around the small room, her heels clicking on the hardwood floor. "I don't like this idea." Richard slumped into a worn armchair, running a hand through his already rumpled hair.

"Why not?"

It's too dangerous.

"What will we eat? What will happen to our pharmacy?" Alice asked, while stroking Bobby's hair with one hand and biting her fingernails with the other.

God has already provided for you. He gave you a freezer full of food, my old rifle, and the wilderness that has always had plenty of game. It's a perfect place for young men to explore and discover biology, geography, and the natural habitats. It's a young man's paradise.

Everyone sat in silence, overwhelmed.

When you arrive, take off your shoes and wade into the cool water of the mountain spring. Use my old Bible for comfort and read it. We should have been reading it all along. You can also bring your computers, as God has provided a generator for electricity and lights.

Alice was the most upset. Grandpa tried to comfort her and give her hope, even as he secretly mourned his wife. She had been a genuine Christian and had died several years earlier. Why hadn't he listened to her?

If I'm still here, I'll let you know when it's safe for you to return.

***

After three hours of travel, five rest and bathroom breaks, and battling mosquitoes on a hot summer night, the tired travelers stopped at the base of a mountain. Richard considered the health of the refugees traveling with him.

Luke, Richard's oldest son, shucked off his suitcases like a pack mule and slumped to the ground. "Opening day of college football season didn't hurt this bad," he groaned. The rest of the family followed his lead.

"Okay, troops," Richard said. "Fifteen minutes to rest and refresh, then we climb."

"Let's just sleep here tonight," Luke begged. "I'm beat."

We can't, son. The Red Devil can see and smell us, and he's supposed to be able to fly. He's going to be looking for us. Let's go.

Richard believed the Red Devil was clever. The Red Devil would see the group as easy prey if they were out in the open. Once on the mountain trail at night, they would move more slowly but could use the forest for cover.

Richard's mind drifted back to Grandpa John, who had sacrificed himself for his family. Richard prayed, "Lord, be merciful to Dad."

He knew the mountain trail would be slow and tough for Bobby, but Bobby would enjoy the hooting of night owls and the movement of nocturnal animals.

***

When they arrived at the cabin, Bobby prayed and thanked God. His prayer deeply touched his family. That night, peace returned to them.

In the morning, the sun sparkled on tall pines screening blooming honeysuckle vines. The cabin felt like the perfect hideout, safely out of the Red Devil's view.

On a clear day, people on the mountain could see the ocean on one side. On the other side, the jagged rock face of the neighboring mountain came into view. From the cabin, they could easily overlook the town of Stonewall below. From that height, Stonewall's buildings appeared as specks.

White fog drifted over the city as a fluffy, low-hanging cloud slid between the mountains, almost as if it were putting on a show for them. Richard's eyes sparkled at the scene. He leaned forward on the porch railing of the cabin.

Luke found his old telescope, the one he had used for stargazing as a child. He wiped a layer of dust off the lens with his sleeve. He used the telescope to observe Stonewall and his former home.

The family chose Luke as their spy, mainly to keep an eye on the Red Devil. Luke also took plenty of pictures of the night sky for his college astronomy class.

On the second day of their retreat, Luke mentioned that the summer preschool classes had ended—he pointed to the empty schoolhouse visible through the lens—and that only delivery trucks and ambulances were still running in Stonewall.

The Red Devil destroyed the churches and shut down the government buildings in Stonewall. He also tore apart people's homes and looted everything he could find in the rubble. No police remained to patrol Stonewall anymore. Instead, the Red Devil wandered the deserted streets of the town.

At dusk each evening, Grandpa flashed "SOS" with a spotlight in Morse code to warn them it was unsafe to return. His jaw tightened with each precise flash. Luke read the code perfectly.

Who would have guessed that learning Morse code for his Scout communication badge would prove to be so valuable?

***

The family spent years, then months, then weeks in exile, but they gradually adapted to life in the mountains. After he accepted Jesus as his Savior, thirteen-year-old Bobby read the Bible every day. He also kept questioning and searching for his purpose.

Bobby pressed his palms together, his voice barely a whisper, "I pray we can see Grandpa soon. I miss him."

For three years, the family oversaw Bobby's education. He also helped his mother with household chores and chopped firewood for the fireplace.

Bobby asked his father, "Why do I have to wash dishes and make beds?" Bobby scuffed his bare foot on the wooden floor.

We want you to learn how to become an adult and support your own family someday, if that day ever comes.

Bobby nodded, picking at a splinter on the edge of the table. He paused, then asked, "Father, Jesus told me to ask you: would you like to be saved?"

Richard ran his fingers through his hair, his face turning ghostly pale. "Yes, I guess so."

Richard called Alice and Luke into the living room. When they arrived, he explained that God had told Bobby to ask if he wanted to be saved. "Does the rest of the family want to be saved?"

Alice said, "We missed our chance, but I pray each night that Bobby will be saved. He never had that opportunity because we never told him about Jesus." She cried. "Maybe there's hope for him."

Luke agreed with his mother, and Richard bowed his head in shame.

Bobby said, "I pray there is hope for us all." The others looked at him quietly. "In the book of Revelation, people in white robes under the altar wait for others who will die in the service of the Lord and then receive their robes. I believe that, and God has called me to his service."

"What can you do for Jesus, Bobby?" Alice asked again.

"Luke, tell everyone what you told me today," Bobby demanded. "He needs to tell you, regardless of his fear."

Grandpa hasn't signaled us in three days, so I checked the old oak tree in secret but found nothing. I was afraid to tell you.

Everyone was crying.

Bobby declared, "I will end this mess with the Red Devil. The Bible says Christ strengthens me to do all things." He slammed his fist on the table.

His father asked, "You're only thirteen, Bobby. What are you going to do?"

I'll show you, Father. He straightened his shoulders and looked his father in the eyes.

Bobby slipped into his bedroom. His family heard him searching, and he found the slingshot his father had given him for Christmas.

As Bobby walked through the living room, his father asked, "Bobby, where are you headed with that slingshot?"

Come on, join me, he gestured toward the front door.

Richard grabbed Grandpa's old rifle. Luke picked up an axe. Alice took her garden hoe. Together, they headed to Stonewall with Bobby.

After a long walk, they reached the end of Main Street in Stonewall and headed toward where the Red Devil guarded the front entrance.

As they walked down the street, others—who had long survived like animals among the ruins of their homes—armed themselves with whatever they could find and began to follow the convoy.

The Red Devil lay beneath an old oak tree. When Bobby and the town's convoy approached, the Red Devil lifted his head and looked at them.

What do you want, punk?

"I want Jesus Christ to save you with his grace." Bobby raised the slingshot, his hands steady.

The Red Devil chuckled so loudly that the ground shook beneath his feet. "If you and your gang don't leave, I will crush all of you with my feet." The devil began to stand.

Bobby searched under the oak tree for an acorn, picked a big, shiny one, and loaded it into his slingshot. His eyes stayed on the massive Devil.

The Red Devil burst into laughter. "So you think you're a Goliath slayer?" The Red Devil grinned, his teeth like shattered bones. Well now... Let me give you a good target." The Red Devil took a long, deep breath, inhaling sharply, and the rush of air whooshed past.

He puffed out his massive chest. "I'll give you the first shot," he bellowed. He pounded his massive chest with a spiked fist. "Give me the best you've got!"

With trembling arms, Bobby pulled back the slingshot—now loaded with an acorn—as far as he could. Sweat dripped from his chin. He took careful aim and fired, but the acorn didn't move.

Instead, thunder roared, and a lightning bolt shot out from the slingshot. The bolt slammed into the Red Devil's chest like a guided missile.

The Red Devil screamed in horror. He clawed at the glowing bolt. He tried to pull the bolt out with his hands, but it sank even deeper into his chest.

He staggered to one side. His eyes widened in disbelief. "What have you done?" he screamed. He started to fall like a giant tree toward the people standing in the street.

The crowd panicked and scattered to escape the falling Red Devil, but Bobby held his ground.

As he fell to his death, the Red Devil made a final move. He swung his spiked tail at Bobby and tore him apart.

That day, Jesus dressed Bobby in a brand-new white robe.

And what about the people who stayed behind? That day, a small spark of hope returned to Stonewall.

13

Chapter 13

"I WANT IT MY WAY"

A gap in the linen curtain revealed the empty kitchen. Now was his chance. He carefully and quietly took every last barley-and-honey cookie from the clay jar. Mom's heart would break.

He ran to his elementary school and started trading cookies with his friends. He wanted to launch a small business. But what kind of business?

"Let's trade kisses with the girls," Obed said. "Yuck!" Miriam covered her mouth with a hand. "That's a stupid plan. Use your head. Bribe the teacher's pets for test answers."

Judas said, "That's a great idea, but who can we get to approach the teacher's pets?"

"Don't you know girls are the teacher's pets? Boys are clueless," said Miriam. "I know them all; give me the cookies, and I'll handle the details." She enjoyed great success organizing Judas's plan.

At each grade level in the school, a teacher's pet agreed to gather test questions. Those selected students who worked with Judas earned money or received gifts. The grading system collapsed, and for a brief period, Judas ruled as the student kingpin of graft. It all started when Judas stole cookies from home.

The traditional school rigidly enforced its motto: "Check every i and cross every t. Twice." His social status called for a more relaxed attitude than that strict school motto could ever permit.

He suggested to school officials that they relax traditional rules about eating biblically forbidden foods and wearing clothing that follows religious standards. He also recommended allowing boys and girls to socialize during religious holidays. The school rabbis opposed the idea and labeled it satanic.

Judas believed that life's privileges were his right, which fueled a sense of entitlement that closed his eyes to the consequences of selfishness and ambition.

His parents lived extravagantly, so it was natural for Judas to expect only the best. He didn't care that his parents worked hard, trading honestly to earn their wealth.

The conservative, traditionalist headmaster uncovered Judas's organized, money-making scheme. Expulsion immediately followed; the synagogue excommunicated the family.

Excommunication ruined the business. Jerusalem's citizens publicly shamed and continually shunned the Iscariots. Judas didn't care that he had caused the severe punishment, which reflected badly on his parents and their business. He was too privileged and arrogant to see it.

The shaming and shunning left them humiliated and ostracized. Unfortunately, Judas's parents never enforced discipline on him; they hoped that as he grew older, he would recognize his mistakes.

Judas's father, a businessman who traded goods and services, decided to move his family and business to Jericho. Judas felt no remorse for his actions.

Moving the business proved to be a wise decision—the business thrived again. However, Judas's reputation followed him; no other school would accept him. As a result, his parents took charge of his education. They homeschooled young Judas, teaching him self-reliance skills. His father prepared him to take over his role in the business eventually.

Young Judas matured into a cunning manipulator. He rapidly learned what was right and wrong in life and business. His greed for money continued to grow.

***

Years later, the family business prospered in Jericho. Judas's father appointed him to manage marketing and research. However, his father's views on those roles conflicted with Judas's ambitions.

Strategically located near Amman in Jordan, Jericho provided access to Saudi Arabia to the east, Syria to the north, and Egypt to the south through trade caravans. From there, the family expanded the company through import and export trade.

As the family business grew three times larger, Judas was often away. His father, focused on success, didn't notice Judas starting a personal trading business in other countries. Judas used the family trade name without permission and kept all the profits. He planned to take over his father's role in the company gradually.

He remembered conservative teachings from the Psalms: "The LORD is good to all, and his mercy is over all that he has made."

Judas distorted the text. This wealth is justified, he rationalized, and my secret business is righteous. He continued his unconventional methods, growing richer. Judas once again ruled as his own king of business.

Then a royal envoy from Syria visited Judas's father, and Judas's father recognized Mr. Iscariot as a Syrian friend and an official trade partner. The envoy proudly listed his son's accomplishments. Mr. Iscariot's chest swelled—until he heard the details: treachery and deceit fueled his new fortune.

He stared at the man, his pride fading away. Judas loved money and power and always ignored ethics. A cold certainty settled in: Judas would kill him. Mr. Iscariot knew because this was how he had inherited—or taken—control of the company from Judas's grandfather. It brought a curse of sin upon the Iscariot family.

A week after the envoy returned to Syria, Mr. Iscariot called his son to discuss his trade and research business.

Judas detailed his plan, a brilliant strategy (his words) to grow the family's business far beyond anyone's wildest dreams. Pride swelled in his chest; he had made the name Iscariot infamous—a global brand.

He had doubled the family's treasury. The facts spoke for themselves. All he needed was his father's approval, his acceptance of the necessary treachery.

Mr. Iscariot asked, "Where is the family's share of all the profits?" The mood shifted. Nausea grew in Judas's stomach. His father knew.

He scrambled for a response, any response, but his tongue felt thick. "It's my money, not yours. I made that money, not you," he stammered, the words echoing in the heavy silence.

Mr. Iscariot placed his hands on his son's shoulders, tears blurring his vision. "My son, I am proud to see you grow and develop into a businessman." His grip tightened slightly. "But I'm afraid my sins have passed on to you. My lust for money and power drove me to eliminate my father from his family business. You have your own treacherous sin of lust for money and power. My sin continues to curse me through your actions against me."

Again, he placed his hands on his son's shoulders and, with tears in his eyes, said, "Syria's king sent an envoy to welcome me into the global trading world. They praised you, not realizing your treachery against me. You must not gain glory through dishonest means."

Don't you remember the lessons at traditional school? 'Your heart is deceitful above all things and desperately sick; who can understand it?' I would have helped you if you had asked. But money isn't true happiness.

With his hands still on his son, he continued, "I will not let my curse ruin you. I failed in raising you, and now you need harsh medicine. That is why I banish you from our family. You are on your own. I will take over all your business affairs and personal financial accounts. You have no money. I will ask you to leave and learn the lessons you have resisted."

Judas jerked back, and redness spread across his face. Father, you're angry! What are you implying? I've proven myself in business—they lied to you! You and Mother will regret this decision!

***

Satan planted hateful ideas deep inside him. A bitter heart took shape, growing colder each day. Vengeance, that sweet poison, coursed through his veins. He only thought of hurting his father and mother.

They were suffocating traditionalists, weighed down by their beliefs. They rejected the liberal religious ideas of their time; to them, a coming Messiah was just a fantasy. They insisted that the Law of Moses was the only way to earn God's favor.

John the Baptist was everything they despised. The very idea of joining him—of being different—made his parents grit their teeth. They would disown him.

Witnesses described him as a man in the wilderness preaching repentance and baptizing as a sign of it. His rough clothes made of camel hair and his habit of eating locusts and honey—Judas's parents considered it an abomination. John the Baptist upset conservatives every time he announced the coming of the Messiah.

Judas found out that John the Baptist was baptizing people near Jerusalem. He went to the river and waited with others for his turn to be baptized. When it was his turn, John looked at Judas and asked, "Do you ask forgiveness of your sins, and do you confirm your confession by this baptism?"

Judas responded convincingly, "Yes!" He felt nothing for the lie, not a hint of remorse. John the Baptist welcomed Judas into his circle of disciples.

John the Baptist expected his disciples to live as he did, but Judas could only sustain himself on locusts and honey, driven by hatred and a thirst for revenge against his parents.

Without John's knowledge, he started acting as John's frontman. Judas would travel to the next town and prepare the crowd for John's arrival. He charged a small fee for a special spot at the baptism site, and for a little extra, he would arrange for people to touch John as he passed by.

Then he asked his fellow disciples for help with his illegal scheme. He requested their assistance in helping the sick and disabled attend the baptism ceremony. Judas told John's disciples that God approved of his voluntary act of love.

He never mentioned fees to the disciples. He called the scheme his Stretcher of Help Service. Throughout, he collected more fees from families of disabled people without John and the other disciples knowing.

Judas wisely invested his money and became the treasurer for John the Baptist's disciples. He fed the disciples, and when their families needed help, he provided for them as well.

People willingly paid fees to attend the baptism service because Judas told them it was a way to earn God's favor. Although Judas was successful in his business, he was troubled by a pain he couldn't relieve.

King Herod Antipas had darker plans for John the Baptist. John's words, like a dangerous song, still echoed in the marketplace, piercing the air. Herod's wife, a wicked woman, couldn't tolerate them. They took John to the dungeon and silenced him for four long months. No one saw him.

Then, only rumors—a sword cut, a basket. Judas felt his guts tighten in sheer panic. Herod didn't let anyone disagree.

Without John the Baptist present, his disciples disbanded. The disciples of Jesus and their followers grew, and they needed Judas to meet with Jesus to discuss managing their treasury.

Judas's reputation grew due to his service to the community. Jesus needed and accepted Judas's help as treasurer and disciple. However, he also used Judas for a different purpose. Jesus needed one of the twelve to betray him to fulfill the ultimate plan— but only through that person's own intentions.

***

The relationships between the apostles and Jesus were harmonious until Satan once again planted greed, jealousy, and revenge in Judas's willing heart.

Jesus and his disciples went to a wedding in Galilee. Jesus' mother was also there. She told Jesus that the woman's family had run out of wine for the guests.

In Jewish tradition, running out of wine at a celebration would shame the family. So Jesus' mother asked him to perform a miracle and supply the family with wine. Jesus instructed someone to fill six water jars to the brim.

When the family patriarch drank what he thought was water, he detected its rich aroma and then tasted the finest wine he had ever had. The bride's father learned that Jesus had turned water into wine and asked how much he should pay Jesus. But Jesus required no payment.

Judas watched the celebrants drain their cups—the good stuff. A fortune, wasted on these... these beggars. "Unwise," Judas muttered the word, his eyes following the server as they poured another cup. "We could have sold that."

Peter turned his back, staring into the crowd as if he hadn't heard a word.

The tight knot in Judas's chest flared with resentment. He'd put the money to good use, unlike the others.

Judas wondered how he could support Jesus and the disciples without any income from others. This wedding was a great opportunity to make money, but Jesus wasted it.

***

A nobleman named Cephas from Galilee approached Jesus and asked him to travel to Capernaum to heal his son, who was close to death. Cephas urged him strongly, warning that if Jesus didn't come to Capernaum, his son would definitely die.

Jesus knew that crowds grew as they listened to his teachings, but he also understood that many were there for healing, not necessarily for faith or to follow him.

Jesus told Cephas that his faith had healed his son and instructed him to go home. Before Cephas could leave, servants approached and informed him that Jesus had healed his son. Like with the wine, Jesus charged nothing for healing the man's son.

This infuriated Judas. His fists clenched, nails digging into his palms as he watched the nobleman thank Jesus without reaching for a coin purse. He bit the inside of his cheek to hold back a shout.

"I won't make any money." He kicked at a loose stone on the ground, causing it to skitter across the courtyard. "And I can't buy provisions for the disciples if Jesus does not require money for his miracles."

"Jesus told the devil, 'Man does not live by bread alone.' You need to think about that, Judas," Peter said, stepping closer with a furrowed brow full of sincere concern.

Judas clenched his fists at his sides and stared sharply at Peter.

Jesus went to Bethany to visit Mary and Martha's house. There, he allowed Mary to pour expensive ointment on his feet and dry them with her hair.

Judas said, "That oil was worth three hundred shekels! Why didn't we give it to the poor instead of him?" He gestured wildly at Jesus' feet, his voice rising.

Jesus said, "Leave her alone. She has been planning this for a long time."

Jesus didn't look up from his meal, his tone calm.

Judas clenched his teeth and seethed. "I see that Jesus wants the good things, but will not grant us the same privilege." He spun around and stormed out of the room.

After Jesus scolded him, Judas looked for revenge and a way to hurt Jesus, just like he had hurt his father and mother.

Satan didn't pass up the opportunity to plant a revenge scheme in Judas's mind. Judas accepted the idea, a dark smile crossing his lips.

***

Judas went to the headmaster of the traditionalists and struck a deal. The headmaster stroked his long beard, his eyes shining with satisfaction. Although they had long since expelled him from the school, they now shared a common interest. For thirty pieces of silver, while Jesus prayed in the Garden of Gethsemane, Judas would identify Jesus with a kiss. In exchange for his betrayal of Jesus, they decided to punish him for his arrogance.

The conservative traditionalists needed a reason to bring Jesus to trial. They used Jesus' teaching on forgiving sins and his claim to rebuild the temple in three days. Judas provided the perfect reason.

But things didn't go the way Judas had hoped. After the council beat Jesus and mocked him, they took him to King Herod to face punishment, hoping that the sentence would be death. The authorities were forbidden by traditional law to kill Jesus.

When Judas learned that the Roman governor had ordered the soldiers to crucify Jesus, he felt remorse for betraying Him. He returned to the council, threw the thirty pieces of silver on the ground, and begged them to reverse their decision.

Judas truly felt guilty for bearing false witness against Jesus. He never expected they would crucify Jesus.

They told Judas that the Romans had made the decision and wouldn't change it.

What he did to Jesus troubled him, and he reflected on what his father had told him—that he had pushed his own father aside to take control of the family business. His actions had cursed him, and now they had passed on to his son.

At last, Judas realized what he had done. After all these years, guilt overwhelmed him. He covered his face with his hands, tears streaming down between his fingers. He saw no way to redeem himself and went out, hanging himself from a tree.

***

Some believe God set Judas up, but Judas always acted according to his own nature and choices. God allowed him to do so—just as he allows us.

What are your thoughts?

14

Chapter 14

"MY BROTHER'S KEEPER"

Reverend Richard Pearlgate enjoyed his favorite hot tea, a sweet treat. The intercom buzzed, interrupting his moment of relaxation. His secretary told him he had an incoming call from the Central Bank of Moonriver.

Instead of a bank employee's usual greeting, an anonymous female voice said, "I can't take it anymore." A pause. "A large envelope is on my dining room table for your eyes only. I hope you arrive before the police. The front door is unlocked at 221-C Raker Avenue." The call ended.

The voice and tone beckoned him. Familiar. Pearlgate ran the address through his computer records, but nothing appeared. What should he do? He searched his mind for complaints, arguments with parishioners, anything. Who could be in trouble? It sounded dangerously serious. A setup? A trap?

"Why?" he demanded, voice trembling with emotion.

The dusty townsfolk shuffled past small, empty churches, but Achan Church stood out—a respected megachurch with a crowded parking lot. Ten full-time workers—ranging from ministers to maintenance staff—kept the place busy. People called it perfect in the papers. Today, it's a sham; reporters and townspeople use very different words now.

He stood, shrugged into his black trench coat. He grabbed his fedora from the hat rack, adjusted the red feather, and placed it on his gray-haired, half-bald head.

He bowed his head, arms lifted toward heaven. "Jesus, be merciful." Protect me. Unease churned in his stomach as he started walking. He braced himself against the wall, hand flat on the wood, before stepping out the back door.

The sun sank behind storm clouds as he parked his car a block from 221-C Raker Avenue. Rain began to fall as he took the short walk. The storm—the rain—felt like an omen. What will I find at that address?

As he stepped onto the bungalow's front porch, the rain intensified. Lightning flashed, and a thunderclap so loud he flinched, his heart pounding in his chest. The front door was slightly ajar. He froze. A setup? Maybe this woman wanted him inside, ready to scream and accuse the pastor of wrongdoing, or something worse.

Suddenly, a plastic-wrapped newspaper whooshed past his head and collided with the front door, knocking it wide open. He spun around. A newspaper boy was pedaling away on his bike. Great. A witness. The thought sent a jolt of adrenaline through him.

His hands trembled, fear a cold weight in his chest. Every instinct told him to leave. God only knew why he entered the house anyway.

Standing in the living room, he yelled, "Ma'am, are you here?" He repeated the question, voice louder this time. No response. Only the sound of rain hitting the roof of the bungalow. An overturned coffee table, wet coffee stains soaking into the carpet next to a couch pillow—the mess was instantly clear.

The phone felt heavy in his hand. Police, yes, call them. But where's the envelope? Blood pounded in his ears; he moved slowly and cautiously toward the dining area.

There was a large envelope on the dining table, just as the unknown caller described. He shook out the contents, scattering them across the tabletop. Fear began to take hold.

After separating the pictures from the large bank drafts, beads of sweat formed on his forehead. Each picture told a story of a terrible past event. He knew each one, and they revealed the chilling hunger of a serial killer. His signature on each bank draft automatically triggered an audit of the bank records. His legs buckled as he sat in a dining chair. His preacher's mask was crushed.

Who knew this? Who was aware of his past?

The black-and-white photos gazed up at him from the table. He hurriedly arranged them in order, a desperate attempt to regain control. His heart pounded a frantic rhythm against his ribs.

Lord, my God, please forgive me.

Five withdrawal slips, each for $100,000, were followed by a check stub for half a million dollars. His unmistakable signature appeared on every slip and the stub: Paid to the estate of Rudd Mudd.

Anger, hot and sudden, flushed his face. Embezzlement! Church funds! Who? He squeezed his eyes shut, a sharp grimace twisting his features. But I signed them—my hand.

Finally, he took out ten handwritten pages from the envelope. They read:

The envelope's contents would jog my memory, as if I needed help. Every morning, the memory would come back. For your benefit, here's a quick refresher.

A hot August night in Cocklebur Flat. The community leader called every resident, including children, to the mill pond at the head of Bay River.

Most families slogged along the long, miserable, dusty, musty-smelling dirt road. Heat and sweat made us easy targets for mosquitoes. Their bites stung like hellfire, tormenting me with every step.

The dirt road narrowed at the top of the river. The roadside gently rose, offering a comfortable spot to sit and watch the festivities.

A large-bellied man in a long white robe stood on a fish crate. He called the assembly to order with a low, gravelly voice. A red-feathered hat shaded his slightly darkened sunglasses. A full beard and mustache covered the rest of his face.

He told the gathered crowd that they had come to settle some family business. He called for Rudd Mudd's family. Two men led Rudd's wife, two daughters, and son to the front, where they faced the speaker.

Then he called Rudd over. One neighbor brought a footstool and placed it in front of the family. Another pair of neighbors escorted Rudd to the stool and helped him stand, facing the crowd and his family.

With two men tying his hands behind his back, Rudd stood as someone brought horse hobbles and attached them to his legs.

Rudd pleaded, whining for his life. "Please don't do this in front of my family."

"Did you consider Joe's feelings when you caught Rudd with the man's wife in the barn?" the man in white asked.

Rudd's wife sobbed and begged as they blindfolded him. Her cries pierced through the air.

Do you remember the crowd chanting to hang him?

Can you hear his daughters yelling, "Don't hurt our daddy"?

Rudd's family cried out passionately. His son warned the white-robed man, then pleaded with him not to hurt his father. The son warned the man again before falling into desperate pleas.

His son, separated from his mother, ran to hold onto his father's leg.

Can you see your daddy, also dressed in a white robe and red-feathered hat, pulling the little boy's hands away while he clings to his daddy's leg?

Do you hear the crowd cheer when you hand the rope to your dad?

Do you see your daddy throw the rope over the branch of the oak tree, which once stood innocent but now bears the weight of a hanging tree? I hope you remember. I do.

However, the night's main event left a lasting mental scar on me. You both shoved Mr. Rudd off the stool. Oh, how the people cheered. But I cried.

Your daddy told you to grab Mr. Rudd's legs and hang from them to add more weight to the rope and possibly snap his neck. You became the executioner, and you took pride in it.

I have hated you ever since that night. Sometimes, my passion almost drove me to kill you. But how could I? "Vengeance is mine, saith the Lord."

The night was dull until later, when the sheriff's cuffs clicked onto your father's wrists, and they took him to jail.

I'm glad I won't have to see him again.

The entire community showed you mercy because you were just a little boy.

But that probably made you think you could get away with anything. One single, burning prayer kept me going: Find you. Bring you to justice.

Do you remember that August night, Willie Johnson?

Yes, I know who you are.

After that night, my ability to function began to decline. I fought every boy who greeted me.

Church bells made my skin crawl. Public gatherings, family reunions, school assemblies—I couldn't bear them. Mother took me to a psychologist, who explained that a traumatic experience had caused my antisocial behavior. Only a professional could figure that out, not my mother. How pathetic!

After that, you never saw me again. No one did, because I ran away and never came back. I survived on sheer willpower and the anger that surged through my veins. I distanced myself from everyone.

Later, I found out that my mother died from a broken heart, all alone and feeling desolate.

You disappeared and escaped justice.

As I became an adult, I decided to discover who might enjoy a public hanging. Researching your family's background provided me with my first clue.

Your grandmother let me review the family records of births, deaths, and marriages from an old family Bible. Can you imagine when I discovered a certificate of membership for you and your father in a hate-syndicated organization? The situation suddenly became clear; it no longer surprised us.

Your grandmother kept detailed notes. I knew she hated what your dad did; she never missed a chance to tell me. She opposed your father's actions. After your mother died, your grandmother cursed your father's name for bringing you into training to take his place as an enforcer for the hate organization.

Your father's executions shattered her heart. She documented each one, including your executions. She even drew maps of the cemetery where you and your father used to bury the bodies.

Before she died, she gave me her family Bible, along with all the notes and maps she had recorded. Unsure about their accuracy, I double-checked them. They are perfect.

She told me to stop you and bring you to justice, but I didn't know how.

After working at a funeral home for several years, I learned techniques for finding lost graves.

It took me right to each of your father's burial sites. Many newer graves are next to them. You kept using the same cemetery as your hidden burial ground.

Your grandmother also gave the names and dates of each public hanging. Then, about twenty years ago, it all came to a halt.

You moved forward.

After trying many different jobs in various places, my focus narrowed to unexplained deaths among minority communities. Which city has the most? Will it ever satisfy his hunger for murder?

As a result, I moved to Moonriver and got a job at the local bank, but I didn't find what I was looking for until I attended church. As an investment agent and accountant, visiting the bank's most prominent investors is customary. My list includes Achan Church.

You, standing behind the pulpit. A sharp intake of breath, a sudden freeze behind the pew. My stomach curdled, vomit burning my throat. "Fraud. Murderer." I gripped the wood until my knuckles cracked, fighting the urge to rise, to scream it out.

The church's name should have been a clue, but the pieces hadn't fallen into place until now. Like Achan in the Bible, he betrayed God. What a hiding spot.

When I left Achan Church that Sunday, I felt a renewed determination to continue investigating hate crimes and missing persons. My anger fueled my pursuit. Revenge, my reward.

Then, for more than a year, there were no reports of minority murders or disappearances. Unusual. However, I suspected the church might have made it easier for you to find victims.

Years spent tracking you. Years. Then, the attic. My skin crawled, but I pushed through the dark. That small room reeked of old dust and something metallic. "Slaughter room." The evidence was everywhere. Church-sponsored.

I photographed the blood splatter, collected samples, and lifted prints from the knives and clubs. The notebook felt heavy in my hands—every detail secured. It's safe now; I've already given the lock combination and location to the police, and I've placed copies in this envelope.

Yet the evidence, the path to revenge, offered no euphoria. I wept for the Rudd Mudd family. For all the others. Especially the Mudds.

What can I do to help them?

I lost track of them over the years while I was focused on seeking revenge. After forty years, I knew very little about the family.

The local Gazette lay open in my hands, an estate notice glaring off the page. A relative of the Rudd Mudd family asked if anyone had a claim against Sarah Mudd's estate. The will. It all clicked now. Sarah and Rudd.

Suddenly, I came up with a plan. At the very least, I would give the Rudd heirs the overdue compensation they deserved. My fingers clenched the pen as you entered, and I signed all five withdrawal slips and the check without hesitation. Of course, you didn't read or question anything. Not you. A euphoric wave of emotion washed over me!

Excitement, thick and sweet as icing, pulsed through every vein. Tomorrow. The church audit—that blessed nightmare—finally begins. A shiver, sharp and cold, ran down a spine. "Surprise, murderer."

Here's another mystery: I woke up this morning wanting to read my Bible. Was there anyone else who enjoyed revenge this much? Not in these pages.

From your grandmother's Bible, I read about Cain killing his brother, Abel. He asked God, "Am I my brother's keeper?" While your grandmother asked me to bring you to justice, she asked God to save you in Jesus's name. I don't know about God's part, but soon I will have finished mine.

When I hear the creak of the porch boards as you step on them eagerly, I will call the police and go into the bathroom. I will enjoy spurting red, life-giving blood on the walls and floor.

You will open this package I left for you, and at last, horror will surprise you. In death, I rejoice in your downfall, murderer.

But the pain keeps the coward, murderer, from coming and seeing the blood or death, and I rejoice. What could be better than the revenge of a sweet sister's written confession? Especially after her widowed mother unwittingly married your despicable father.

Happiness flows from my soul, but I will see you somewhere on the other side in a place prepared for you and me.

***

Willie Johnson, also known as Pastor Reverend Richard Pearlgate, broke down and began crying.

Then several sirens grew louder, and blue lights flickered through the windows. Willie placed the contents back into the envelope.

The police rushed in.

He sat quietly, gesturing toward the bathroom with his eyes on the floor, tears falling like rain. The police entered the bathroom. One of them quickly returned and asked the preacher if he knew the victim. Willie handed the envelope to the detective.

"Yes, she is my sister, Sally Anne Johnson."

15

Chapter 15

"SECOND CHANCE"

Rain gutters overflowed, and rainwater flooded the streets; lightning flashed across the sky as thunderclaps shook the ground. Chief of the Detective Division, Jimmy, unfolded his knees from the battered sedan. The younger detectives dispersed to the front of the building without a word, leaving him in the rear alley as usual, standing on the sidewalk in the torrential rainstorm.

The detective unit burst through the front door of the hotel apartment. From the fourth-floor window, they yelled down to warn Jimmy about the suspect escaping. Jimmy strained his ears, but the sound of rain pounding on the asphalt and the crack of thunder completely muffled their shouts.

He heard the fire escape rattle. He turned and looked up. A man jumped to the ground. Then two shots—bang, bang! A static hum filled Jimmy's world. Aimless and spectral, he drifted through time and space.

What happened to Jimmy? Is Jimmy dead? Where is he going through time and space?

***

At age six, Jimmy was hiding under tables and sketching their shoes in a spiral notebook; he called it his case file. Solomon's display of judgment in the case between two women over a child encouraged Jimmy to learn everything he could about King Solomon.

His mother would find his notebooks and smile. "Solomon himself couldn't piece together a better story," she'd murmur, a silent hope in her heart. Years later, a gold shield sparkled on the chest of Chief Detective Jimmy Whorton.

Now, he stood between the caskets of a man and his wife in a busy mortuary.

His reflection in the polished wood of the casket lid revealed a stranger's eyes staring back from beneath the vestments. His hand, clutching a leather-bound Bible, trembled. His gaze blurred the gold leaf. He felt suffocated by the heavy velvet stole. He ran his hand through unfamiliar hair. "What the heck! Who or what am I?"

He caught the eye of a passing attendant with a sharp nod. "How much longer?" he mouthed. She shook her head, a sad line crossing her lips. "It's over," her expression conveyed. Jimmy closed his eyes and whispered a prayer so softly that only God could hear it.

The deceased couple's only child, an eight-year-old girl, sat in the front row. Alice Rae, her small frame trembling, started to whimper, "No, please! Don't let him! I want my mommy and daddy!"

The man grabbed the little girl's hand, pulled her out of her chair, and dragged her away. She cried and begged Jimmy to help. Tears streamed down her face; she reached toward Jimmy, her chest heaving with silent sobs. Jimmy protested, telling the man to stop. The man continued walking away with the girl as she sobbed and pleaded for help.

Jimmy's police training kicked in. He strutted forward and grabbed the man's coat to stop him.

The stranger, a tall man wearing a Stetson and cowboy boots, bowed his head with wide eyes and charged forward, nearly knocking Jimmy over.

Jimmy tried not to twitch.

I'm the little girl's uncle, Charlie from Texas, and I'm her closest kin. He then kept dragging the child toward the door, paused, looked back, and said, "I'll see you tomorrow at the church for the reading of the will. And don't get in my face again."

After the audience left, many funeral attendants shook their heads in sadness, saying, "So sorry," because they knew the little girl's deceased parents.

Jimmy crumpled to the floor, wrapping an arm around his stomach, his face a mask of pain as he let out a groan. He stared at the minister's clothing on his body, a wave of disorientation washing over him. The room felt unfamiliar, his own name a phantom on his tongue while delivering a funeral sermon. Pretending to be sick is the only way out of the unknown dilemma.

A beautiful lieutenant from the Clarkston Police Department knelt beside the impostor pretending to be Pastor Roy Sabinto, the local Anglican church's pastor. "Are you all right?" she asked.

"No!" Pastor Sabinto snapped.

He sat up, leaning on his elbows. He tapped his temple. "A year ago, I stumbled down some steps. Now... some days are foggy." He sighed, looking away. "Things have not been the same since. At times, I black out for hours and wake up wondering who I am."

"Where am I?" Roy asked. "And who are you?"

The policewoman moved closer. She placed her fingers on his face to lift his eyelids, looked into them, then leaned in to smell his breath. "You don't seem to be on anything. You must be having one of those episodes."

Then Lieutenant Marsha Garcia gently massaged Pastor Roy's shoulders. Her fingers eased the tension from his muscles, and a soft sigh escaped her lips. "You don't remember anything about yourself or me?"

Roy didn't answer her question. He looked at her, the question hanging in the air between them, like a blank wall in his mind.

I'm thirsty and too old for this.

"Old!" responded Marsha. According to your driver's license, you are thirty-eight, the same age as me, "Pastor Sabinto," Marsha countered, a slow smile playing on her lips. "You didn't seem tired last night in my apartment."

"How do you know all that?" he muttered.

Marsha's gaze fixed on him. "Don't you remember? I'm a member of your church, and we're dating."

Roy smiled as he reached out and gently touched her cheek. "At least I have good taste in lovely women."

Marsha's smile grew wider.

***

Pastor Roy sat in the church conference room when Uncle Charlie entered, still wearing his Stetson and boots from the night before, dragging a little girl who wailed and dug her heels into the carpet.

Bishop Wooster, the church lawyer, and Lieutenant Marsha followed.

Marsha gestured for Pastor Roy to follow her into the hallway, where she revealed details of the Monroe murder case. Lewis and Alice Ruth Monroe, parents of young Alice Rae, were killed by large insulin injections despite not having diabetes. The autopsy officially ruled their deaths a homicide.

Uncle Charlie inherits nothing from his wealthy brother's estate. Alice, the young girl, receives the entire fortune. The church is Alice's guardian and trustee until she turns twenty-one. Do you see the picture?

Roy nodded, "It may get messy in there."

Bishop Wooster gave his opening statement as Roy and Marsha reentered the conference room. Then, the attorney read the wills of Lewis and Alice Ruth Monroe.

Skip the nonsense and get to what the kid and I understand.

The attorney kept reading, a twitching muscle in his jaw as Uncle Charlie's face reddened. The attorney lowered his glasses, peering over the rims at Uncle Charlie.

"First, you get nothing and are not a blood relative," he stated. Your relationship to Mr. Lewis stems from your marriage to his first wife, your mother. She had you with another man before she married Lewis.

Furthermore, the court does not recognize you as Alice Rae's guardian. As of this will's reading, the church now holds legal guardianship of her until she turns twenty-one. Therefore, I ask that you relinquish your control over Alice Rae.

Uncle Charlie snatched a Bible from the conference table and hurled it at the wall. He stood there, glaring. "I didn't want the little pest anyway. You and your bunch of hypocritical holy pretenders will pay for robbing me."

He paced angrily, then kicked a hole in the wall with a loud thud from his silver-toed boots and stormed out, slamming the door behind him.

Marsha turned to Bishop Wooster. "Could I keep Alice Rae until suitable foster parents are assigned?"

Bishop Wooster raised an eyebrow and smiled.

"Or if suitable foster parents are not found . . . "Marsha paused in thought. "I would like to submit adoption papers myself ... if it pleases the court."

Wooster's smile widened. "I believe it just might please the court."

***

Lieutenant Marsha Garcia and little Alice Rae entered a two-bedroom apartment on the second floor of the Anglican Church Convent. When Alice and Marsha stepped inside the tiny apartment, Alice screamed, "Look out!"

A thud echoed as Marsha's body collapsed, her head striking the hardwood with a dull crack.

Within seconds, women in the convent responded to the child's scream and hurried into the room. Several women assisted Marsha, while others ran to the open window leading to the fire escape. They saw a man in a Stetson shove Alice Rae into an old yellow Lincoln before speeding away.

Pastor Roy arrived after hearing the commotion. The convent nurses had revived Marsha and laid her on her bed. She told Pastor Roy what had happened. The other ladies told him about the man who had gone down the fire escape and driven off in the yellow Lincoln. Later, several Clarkston police detectives arrived to investigate the little girl's kidnapping.

Pastor Roy provided a name and asked them to contact the San Francisco police." The detectives leaned forward, exchanging glances to show their curiosity.

Pastor Roy told them, whether it was true or not, that he barely remembered, but over the years, he often heard people confess their sins. However, the confidentiality of the process prevented him from sharing details.

Pastor Roy said, "If I remember correctly, the name of that person is Smiling Charlie. He had a history of kidnapping, murder, and burglary—as in this case."

Within hours, police detectives identified Smiling Charlie Sykes' locations.

The San Francisco Police Department confirmed the modus operandi and verified the old yellow Lincoln registered to Charlie Sykes of Appleboro, a San Francisco suburb.

The landlord said Charlie had paid two months' rent in advance and left three weeks earlier, bound for the East Coast. Charlie told the landlord he had inherited a large sum of money. Then he drove off in his yellow, late-model Lincoln.

The Clarkston Airport reported that someone had abandoned the yellow Lincoln; the plane bound for San Francisco had departed four hours earlier. The Clarkston Police Department notified the San Francisco Police Department to detain him.

***

The next day, Pastor Roy knocked on Marsha's room door at the church convent. She invited Pastor Roy in with a soft, friendly tone. Roy left the room door open as he entered. Marsha asked him to close the door, but he insisted it remain open to avoid misinterpretation of his visit.

Marsha's breath hitched, and she took an involuntary step back, her eyes wide as she processed his unwavering resolve.

"You've changed in the last three nights." A soft smile touched Marsha's lips. She sat beside him, gently took his hand, and stroked his hair, her gaze warm. "Those are the sweetest words anyone has ever spoken to me. However, I don't care what people think is going on. I know you are a gentleman."

Pastor Roy pulled Marsha aside. "Accompany me to Bishop Wooster," he whispered, his eyes fixed on the floor. "I need to unburden myself."

Marsha pulled her hand away from Pastor Roy's and stepped back. "Is it something terrible?" she asked, her voice strained.

Roy smiled, looked at Marsha, and said, "Probably something weirder."

They entered the bishop's office and sat down in front of his executive desk. Bishop Wooster offered his usual "good morning" greeting. He narrowed his eyes and raised his eyebrows, looking directly at Pastor Roy. "Tell me your story."

Pastor Roy hung his head, ashamed to meet Marsha's or Bishop Wooster's gaze. His eyes filled with tears. Roy wiped at his eyes with a trembling hand. A choking sound escaped his throat; words evaded him.

The bishop tried to comfort Roy with words, reciting passages from the Holy Scriptures about a troubled soul. Finally, Pastor Roy gathered enough courage to speak. "I'm not Pastor Roy Sabinto. My name is Jimmy Whorton . . . or at least I think it is, maybe. Or it could have been."

Jimmy Whorton died two years earlier in San Francisco while on a stakeout. He was trying to catch Smiling Charlie Sykes, a burglar and a murderer.

Being rendered speechless, the other two stared at him.

At first, I didn't realize any of this... this... until I appeared as Pastor Roy at the funeral service two days ago. I have regained my past recorded memories and can recall them in detail. What's even crazier is that I vividly remember Pastor Roy's memories.

Marsha yelled, "All of them?"

"Yes, Plum Quat."

Marsha's face turned red as she looked down in shame.

Bishop Wooster looked cold, pale, and quiet, like a gray stone statue standing in a graveyard. He blinked, regaining a little color in his cheeks. He shook his head and told Marsha and Roy that he had never heard of such a phenomenon except for the Lord Jesus Christ.

Roy insisted that Bishop Wooster verify his story with the San Francisco Police Department. Bishop Wooster asked Roy and Marsha to wait in the hallway while he made the call to San Francisco.

Within minutes, Bishop Wooster spoke with Chief Detective Davis by phone. After their conversation, Bishop Wooster sat alone, praying. After what felt like an eternity, Bishop Wooster called Roy and Marsha back into his office. He handed Roy the phone with Chief Davis's number. "Call him; He wants to talk to you."

"Jimmy here," Roy said.

Roy listened as Detective Davis spoke.

Then Roy said, "The address is 123 Neck Road, Apartment building, Fourth floor, Room 409. My badge number is 23369, and my supervisor is Russell. The team that night consisted of you, Clue, Syborg, Thomas, and me. I guarded the rear of the building."

Pastor Roy handed the phone back to Bishop Wooster. The bishop told Detective Davis he would carry out the plan as requested and ended the call.

Bishop Wooster told Marsha and Roy, "This is diabolical, unheard-of, crazy. And it will get crazier. Above all else that may happen, do not speak about your identity to anyone except the San Francisco police."

The silence in the room felt heavy; Marsha wrung her hands, and Roy stared intently at the floor.

"Roy, you will leave on the first flight out to San Francisco tomorrow." Wooster paused. "Marsha, pack a suitcase. You will accompany him as a police exchange officer. Your patrol department approved the plan earlier with San Francisco."

"As for you, Roy, or whoever you are, you are on a sixty-day sabbatical attending a police training course at the San Francisco Police Department." Wooster slowly shook his head. "Let us pray for God's mercy."

***

The four-hour flight from Clarkston to San Francisco felt endless. Marsha's questions flowed nonstop, each one testing Roy's patience. Still, he answered them all clearly, keeping his voice calm as he explained his downfall.

Roy, what's going to happen in San Francisco? I have a feeling Davis might arrest you when we get there, she lowered her voice. I'm glad I packed my 357-caliber pistol.

I didn't bring a gun, and I don't have one. God protects me. I'd rather rescue little Alice Rae anyway. It would be wonderful if Smiling Charlie let me share the gospel of Christ with him.

A terrible rainstorm rolled in as the plane was descending for landing. The plane rocked and shook amid the wind, thunder, and lightning, but it landed safely.

Chief Davis greeted them upon arrival, and instead of arresting Roy, told them to get into the police cruiser quickly. From the front seat, he turned and said, "Charlie Sykes and Alice Rae have just entered the hotel apartment. We want you to be there when it goes down."

Roy shook his head, as if caught in a time loop. The same event couldn't be happening again. Lightning flashed, thunder cracked, and rain pounded the glass.

Chief Davis asked, "You sure you're Jimmy Whorton?"

"No, I am Pastor Roy Sabinto in this body."

Roy, or Jimmy, experienced a strong sense of déjà vu when Chief Davis told Pastor Sabinto and Marsha to watch the fire escape ladder at the back of the apartment building.

The fire escape is Charlie's only way out. The team broke down the apartment door. Sure enough, Charlie left Alice Rae behind, jumped out of the rear apartment window, and scrambled down the fire escape.

When Smiling Charlie reached the bottom of the fire escape ladder, Marsha yelled, "Halt!" Charlie held the ladder with one hand, his gun in the other, aimed straight at Roy's head.

How many times must I kill you?

Bang! Bang!

Still smiling, Charlie lay dead in the dark San Francisco alley. Lt. Garcia holstered her gun.

Roy was left speechless. None of this seemed real.

He and Marsha looked at each other in the pouring rain.

After a few minutes, Alice Rae sprinted around the building and down the alley, with a stakeout officer close behind. She threw herself into Roy's arms, her small body trembling with an intensity that took his breath away. "Daddy!"

Pastor Roy could only stare, the word echoing through the downpour.

Rain plastered Alice Rae's hair to her face. Roy's rough thumb gently swept the damp strands from her eyes. "I'm not your daddy," he managed, the words catching in his throat, "but I wish I could be."

Little Alice's piercing eyes, sharp and steady, fixed on his. "I can make that happen."

Put me down.

Alice placed her feet back on the wet sidewalk.

In the heavy rain, Alice Rae reached into her pants pocket. Her hand came out holding a cheap plastic finger ring—the kind you find in a gumball machine.

She pressed it into Pastor Roy's palm.

Then Alice took Marsha's hand and pulled her close to Roy.

Alice looked at Pastor Roy. "It is up to you," she said, her voice cutting through the pounding rain. "Package deal."

The rain hammered down. The deceased criminal lay still on the pavement. Other officers gathered, watching with a heavy curiosity. A jumble of thoughts and memories, whether his own or not, collided in Pastor Roy's mind. It seemed irrelevant.

Finally, he took a deep, shuddering breath, looked at Marsha, and knelt in the muddy water. "Will you marry me?"

16

Chapter 16

"FREEDOM"

Philomena and her family huddled under their kitchen table as enemy howitzers bombarded Ramah. Each blast shook the house, and the dust from the ceiling settled on the tabletop. The foul smell of fear filled the air.

Philomena screamed, "What's happening, Father? Father, are we going to die?"

Philomena flinches as a cupboard door swings open, plates crash, and something shatters at her feet. She holds her mother tightly, worried that the upcoming explosion might harm them. She closes her eyes tightly and grips her apron.

Her father tried to comfort them, holding Philomena and her mother. Kyra prayed for God's deliverance. Machine-gun fire swept across the street, and screams and shouts never ceased.

King Habin's commander, Sera, ruled through fear. The more lives he took, the more the survivors' spirits shattered.

His modern army—tanks, wheeled cannons, and heavily armed troops—swept through town after town. Sera's troops slaughtered civilians armed with swords and old rifles. Philomena catches a glimpse through a cracked window: a neighbor falls, and an old gun slips from his hands onto the street.

As homes burned and bodies piled up, a brief lull provided a chance to escape. Crowds fled Ramah, leaving behind the injured and elderly to die. A child cries over his deceased parents.

***

Philomena's father sent her and Kyra to his sister's house in Lebanon.

With her fist clenched at her side, Philomena asked, "Why, father— can I fight? Someone has to die so our people can live in freedom. After ensuring his family was safe, Philomena's father joined a makeshift community militia. Enemy soldiers soon killed him in battle.

The Tatchells, part of Philomena's aunt's family, took them in even though they could hardly feed themselves. They had already escaped Ramah during one of Habin's earlier campaigns. Poverty and hunger defined those years.

To support everyone, Philomena worked and grew up with a constant ache from an empty stomach. Kyra taught her how to make candles and the secret of camel-hair wicks that burned for days. Before the war, Philomena's father had prospered from this craft, supplying religious communities with candles for ceremonies and emergencies. The candle shop's scent comforts Philomena, reminding her of her father and his shop.

Electric lights had weakened this trade over time, but Philomena prayed daily for God's blessing so she could feed her mother and help the Tatchells. Eventually, her business grew and prospered. People came to see her as a wise leader and a woman who talked with God.

Then Kyra suddenly died, leaving Philomena to manage the shop alone. Through hard work and careful choices, she continued to thrive and repaid the Tatchells for their support. Many nights, sleep evaded her.

Philomena went back to the hill country of Ephraim, her mother's hometown, and buried her beneath a tall palm tree. Travelers, caravans, and armies stopped at the palm for water from the cool spring that fed the oasis.

Friends and foes alike received Philomena's hospitality. Many later returned seeking her advice and to purchase fruit. Over time, people began to see her as a wise sage, and they believed God's Spirit rested on her.

One Sabbath, a stranger in a Jeep saw Philomena worshiping by the spring with a small group. He watched them finish and then brought her gifts of food, money, and clothing. She looked familiar to him. A stirring in his spirit told him there was some deep connection. He stepped out of his Jeep and walked toward her, hoping his uniform wouldn't make her think he served Sera.

He greeted her. She turned and saw a tall soldier in uniform, gun at his side. Her first instinct was to step back. His warm smile and calm voice eased her fear.

"Who are you?"

"My name is Othniel. I lead the resistance."

"Where are you from?"

"Ramah."

Could she be the childhood love he'd lost when Sera's bombardment forced his family into exile? Silently, he prayed, "God, let it be."

"Cricket?" he asked. "Is it you?"

She stared. "Oh-Otto?"

Yes. Alive, and right in front of you.

Othniel told her that her father had become a spy for the resistance. His own father had sent the family to Egypt, where they later learned that both men had died defending Ramah. Philomena held his hands tightly. "They died so others could live free."

"The Egyptian army trained me as a soldier," Othniel said. "God sent me back to drive out the invaders. Somehow, that path led me here."

Their childhood affection quickly grew into mature love and a shared goal to free their homeland from King Habin. They married, and Philomena danced at her wedding for the freedom Ramah would soon enjoy.

Under Othniel's training, she learned to fight. They became partners in both battle and love.

Othniel rediscovered the God his mother had once told him about as Philomena taught him to pray. Their reputation as warriors and spiritual leaders spread far and wide. Rebels, mercenaries, and villagers joined them, and a freedom army grew.

Soon, word of this resistance reached King Habin. One day, Philomena returned from her candle shop and called for Othniel. There was no answer. His Jeep was outside, but the house was empty. She circles the Jeep, feels the hood still warm. Where is he?

She started asking neighbors when there was a knock at the door. A neighbor handed her a sealed envelope. "A child asked me to bring this to you," the woman said.

Philomena sat down, her hands trembling; she opened it. Inside, she discovered a red note labeled, "King Habin of Ganhan." A tear dripped onto the page as she broke the seal.

It read: The executioner will hang your husband in Ramah jail for treason. I will execute you as well unless you come to me in two nights and dance before me for mercy. If you please me, I will take you as my servant and may spare your life. King Habin

Philomena called the rebel leaders to the large palm tree, then retreated to a secret spot near the oasis to fast and pray. After a day, they summoned her. She read the king's message aloud. They responded with anger, insisting she must not go.

"We all have to be willing to die so others can live free," she said. "But tonight is not my time to die."

Silence fell.

God has given me a plan, she continued. I'll go to the king and agree to dance and sing for him, appealing to his desire for a woman. I'll insist on a grand party in the great hall while I perform, so his followers can praise him for conquering me, his female enemy.

While the celebration continues, you'll send a small strike team to overpower the remaining guards at the jail.

Afterward, the king and I will go to his private chamber. Drunk and exhausted, he'll fall asleep as I sing to him. I'll have long hairpins in my clothes and tear my gown into strips to tie him to the bed.

From his balcony, I'll signal you to storm the jail. Then I'll wait in Othniel's Jeep for the alarm. When Commander Sera learns I've escaped in it, he'll pursue us with his forces. I'll meet you at the River Kishon.

When we see Sera approaching, we'll retreat to Mount Tabor. At sunrise, we'll attack his army from behind, with their backs to the river.

I walk by faith, trusting that my God will keep His promise to defeat our enemies.

***

That night, guards took Philomena into a lively banquet hall filled with music, drinks, and women. They made her kneel before King Habin. He called for silence and introduced her as the evening's entertainment.

"Tonight," he said, "you will watch our female enemy grovel at my feet, hoping to save her pathetic husband with her dancing and singing. If she pleases me, I may commute his death to hard labor."

Later, I will check whether she can serve her king in private. Let this be a warning to anyone who rebels against King Habin of Ganhan. Music!

The party raged until morning. After more than five hours, sweat pouring into her eyes, Philomena collapsed mid-song. Drunk on his throne, the King slumped over until the guards shook him awake and told him she had fallen.

"Good," he muttered.

He staggered over. Guards carried Philomena and followed him to his bedroom, then were dismissed. He ordered her to sing and dance again and flopped onto his bed. Within minutes, his eyes began to droop. Philomena stopped dancing but continued singing softly.

As she sang, she slipped long hairpins from her clothes and set them on the bed, then tore her gown into strips. Her lullaby helped keep him subdued as she tied and pinned his arms, legs, and clothes to the bed.

For a moment, she looked at him, helpless and alone, feeling the urge for revenge. She checked his clothes and found a six-inch knife hidden in his boot. She lifted it over his throat—the blade then froze.

In her heart, she heard: Do not kill. Tears welled in her eyes. "It isn't fair, Lord," she whispered. "I see the faces of the dead. Let me avenge their deaths."
"You must rise above vengeance," the inner voice replied.

Philomena removed her socks, climbed onto the bed, and shook the king awake. He tried to cry out but found himself bound with ropes and pins, with Philomena hovering above him, knife in hand. When he opened his mouth, she stuffed her socks in it and ran.

She burst from the bedroom, signaled the rebels to attack the jail, and sprinted toward the hidden Jeep, shouting to draw the guards after her. When they found their king pinned to his bed, they sounded the alarm.

The Jeep coughed but wouldn't start. A guard reached for her door just as the engine roared to life. The Jeep lurched, dragging him until he fell away.

Philomena sped toward the River Kishon. At the river, she ordered, "Light as many campfires as you can. We must look lazy and unprepared. At sunrise, when Sera's army comes and finds no one here, they'll think we ran and won't be ready. Othniel told her that if she believed this was God's plan, she had to stand with them in the coming fight.

"Gladly," she said, "if I can sing and dance for God's deliverance afterward." They left their tents and fires and withdrew to Mount Tabor.

Sera's army stormed into the empty camp with guns blazing, tanks rumbling through the soft river sand. Seeing the abandoned tents and burning fires, Sera sneered, "The cowards fled into the dark."

He arranged a celebration, and they drank and rejoiced until dawn. As the sun rose behind them over the River Kishon, Philomena and Othniel led a sudden charge from Mount Tabor, surprising the invaders with the rebels' battle cries.

Tank guns fell silent, and the fight moved to close quarters. Othniel and Philomena spun in tandem like a double pinwheel, swords cutting through Sera's soldiers. Half the army broke ranks and fled, including Commander Sera.

Othniel's rebels throw their helmets in the air, celebrating victory.

Some say a woman named Jael hid Sera in her tent, fed him, and kept him hidden from the rebels until he fell asleep—then drove a tent peg through his skull. On the battlefield, the rebels erupted in celebration.

Philomena climbed onto an abandoned tank to sing and dance. God had kept His promise. By His grace, God freed Ramah. "How could life be better?" Othniel asked. A gunshot crackled in the distance. Heads turned. Someone shouted, "Look!" and pointed at Philomena. She fell from the tank.

Othniel rushed to her and lifted her head into his arms. "No, God! Please, no—not Philomena." Barely able to speak, she grasped his hand, looked into his eyes, and whispered, "One life taken, so many may be free."

17

Chapter 17

"BORN IN FIRE"

Joe Davis lifted the neck string of his rubber apron over his head and tied the waist string around his back. He tugged the knot tight against his spine. He grabbed his elbow-length black gloves and slid them on, then lowered his protective goggles over his eyes. He wiped a smudge from the left lens with a gloved thumb.

He checked the thermometer on the cremation furnace: 1,400°F.

Just perfect for cooking.

Joe worked as the crematory operator for the regional university hospital system. He carried out the grim task of burning rejected human body parts, aborted babies, and unclaimed deceased prison inmates. He glanced at the gurney; his reflection distorted in the steel surface.

Unaware of the stories behind any of the removed body parts, lifeless babies, and rejected inmates, Joe imagined tragic backstories for each one. He pressed a hand to his chest, feeling the heavy thump of his heart. Sometimes, emotion overwhelmed Joe when he thought about these stories.

Joe's job made him lonely; maybe that's why he wanted it. A crematory operator was the only work a recluse like Joe could handle. People teased him from childhood to adulthood for being of mixed blood, and he avoided this teasing and judgment by staying out of sight.

When they appeared together in public, others often looked down on his wife. Their voices were filled with contempt because she dared to marry a "half-breed." Joe Davis thought the job as a cremation operator was a perfect fit.

While loading the tray into the furnace, Joe removed the name tags from each bag containing parts or bodies. He opened each bag to verify that the contents matched the ID tags. After Joe loaded the tray halfway with body parts, he filled the remaining half with aborted babies. But today, something unusual happened.

The hospital had prepared only one baby for cremation. He opened the bag and looked at the baby inside — a beautiful baby boy with all his fingers and toes intact, lying motionless. Why did they abort the little boy? Was it for health reasons? To satisfy his curiosity, Joe removed the baby from the black bag to check for injuries. He found none.

Joe began to guess and imagine all the tragic reasons someone might abandon a beautiful little child. His thoughts shifted to family members crying and mourning their little boy's death. He could only imagine their agony, pain, and deep sorrow. A tear fell from Joe's eye, landing on the little boy as he was placed back into the terrible black bag.

Did the parents see abortion as just convenient? Joe kicked at a stray piece of medical tape on the floor. Maybe the mother or father didn't want to deal with an extra life. Or perhaps the mother was overwhelmed by rape, poverty, or other hardships. He ran a gloved hand over the edge of the steel furnace door, the metal cold under his touch. Joe would never be allowed to know, so it shouldn't matter to him, and probably couldn't, even if he wanted it to.

Joe opened the superhot furnace door and slid the stainless-steel tray into the blazing fire. He closed the door and sat on a stool, waiting for the hungry flames to consume the carcasses and turn them to ash.

Joe buried his face in his hands, and his shoulders shook with silent sobs. He needed answers, praying to God about why babies had to die. He needed answers.

After thirty years of marriage, Joe and his wife, Angel, had no children. Joe told himself it wasn't fair. Joe and Angel might be financially poor by social standards, but they were wealthy in love. Lost in his pity party, he suddenly snapped out of his deep thoughts. What's that noise? Joe couldn't tell whether he actually heard a noise or just imagined it.

He heard it again.

It couldn't have been a baby's cry. Joe was the only person nearby.

Then a third time, Joe heard a baby's cry.

Jumping to his feet, rubbing the peephole glass, and looking into the burning inferno, he saw that the ugly black bag had fallen off the table to the bottom of the furnace.

It wiggles.

Shocked stiff by what he heard and saw, Joe fell into desperation.

He raced to the emergency gas shutoff valve on the wall and slammed it shut. With the fire out, he ran back to the furnace and opened the vent-release valve to vent the superheated air up the chimney.

Not waiting for the furnace to cool, Joe grabbed two hand towels and wrapped his hands in them. He released the door lever without thinking about the risk of injury from the superhot furnace and snatched it open. He bent over, reached inside the stove, and grabbed the black bag in one quick motion, ignoring the intense burning of his eyebrows, the hair on his arms, and the tip of his nose.

He took the towels from his hands to smother the flames on the black bag; it was on fire. Since the fire had weakened the bag, Joe tore it open by hand.

There it was: a squirming, hungry, crying, chubby baby boy. Joe picked him up and cuddled the little guy to soothe him.

The father naturally wants to protect his child, so Joe found a latex glove in his desk drawer and a bottle of chocolate milk in his lunch pail. He poked a hole in one of the glove's fingers, poured in the milk, and had the baby suck on the glove finger like a baby bottle. The little fellow drank almost all of Joe's chocolate milk.

After the baby finished his snack, Joe tried to burp him. He was very successful, but he didn't expect the baby to have a bowel movement and urinate at the same time. Joe ended up covered from his arms to his shoes in a wet, sticky, foul-smelling mess.

Now what?

After the staff processed and filed all the legal papers, they officially declared the baby dead. If Joe kept the baby, no one would find out. The baby quickly fell asleep in a makeshift cradle Joe made from a cardboard box in the cremation storeroom. Then he finished the cremation. Now he needed to plan an escape so no one would see the baby as he left for home.

***

Joe parked his car behind his house, at the end of the block, across from an old, abandoned fire tower. It was nice and secluded. The backyard was for washing the car. But today, the parking spot was perfect for sneaking the baby into the house.

The refrigerator was the first stop on the way to a fresh, warm feeding of cow's milk. Joe's wife was busy cleaning a neighbor's house. After placing the makeshift cardboard cradle on the dining table, he warmed the milk in a small pot on the stove.

With a quick switch from the old latex to a new one, he poured warm milk into the clean glove, just in time for the baby's hungry cry. Joe sat at the kitchen table and fed the child. He took pride in his fatherly responsibility to provide for his son.

As Joe fed the child, the child looked into Joe's eyes. Joe spoke cheerful gibberish to him.

The back porch screen door squeaked, and his wife entered the kitchen. She dropped her purse, stopping in her tracks as she stared. Her face went pale.

"Hi, dear," Joe said. "Look what I found in the cooker today."

Angel fainted and collapsed on the floor.

Joe quickly placed the child back in the cardboard cradle and grabbed water from the sink to splash on Angel's face, reviving her slightly.

Groggy, shocked, and confused, she asked, "Where'd you get the child?"

Telling his story with enthusiasm, he called the day's event "A Child Born in Fire." Angel sat quietly, running her fingers through her hair and shaking her head.

She looked at Joe. "Do you know how much trouble you are in?"

"None." He took a long sip of his coffee.

What do you mean, none? She half rose from her chair, her voice rising.

They've already filed all the official papers for the child. He is unclaimed, deceased, and unnamed. I have done nothing wrong.

Have you reported this to the university officials and your supervisor? She wrung her hands, her eyes darting toward the makeshift cradle.

Angel wiped a hand across her forehead, leaving a smear of sweat. No. And if I did, they'd take the baby away from us. What they don't know won't hurt them because they don't want any trouble.

Angel said, "Give me our baby." She held out her arms, a desperate plea in her eyes.

***

Everything was perfect for two months until little Joe Jr. came down with a high fever. They took little Joe to a neighborhood clinic operated by a local church. A nurse practitioner diagnosed little Joe with a common childhood illness and then prescribed an antibiotic.

The nurse asked Joe if he had health insurance through the university to help cover the medical bill. He didn't respond. Instead, he paid the bill in cash. The nurse noted the child's heritage in little Joe's record as a concern.

The next day, their pastor from the local church stopped by for a visit. When Angel answered the doorbell, she didn't invite the pastor inside; she spoke to him through the screen door. Her hands tightened on the frame.

She asked the minister to excuse her hesitation to greet a visitor, saying she wasn't feeling well. Slightly offended, the minister was confused by her sudden illness, as he knew his wife had seen her at the grocery store buying baby formula that morning.

Before Joe got home from work that afternoon, a neighbor named Angel called, complaining that a baby had been crying late the night before and had woken them.

Angel told the woman she was babysitting her grandchild overnight, and the baby was having gas pains. She hung up the phone, a deep sense of relief settling in her chest.

They would bring the child to a hotel if he started crying again.

The neighbor doubted Angel's explanation because Angel had always told her and the other neighbors that she and Joe had no children. If that were true, how could they have grandchildren? The neighbor contacted the county Child Protection Agency and reported the baby crying, along with the strange story Angel shared.

When Joe got home from work, he saw Angel crying. Her eyes were red-rimmed, and her face was blotchy. Sitting in a rocking chair and rocking little Joe, she whispered, "They're closing in, but they'll never take my baby from me." Her hand turned white as she gripped the arms of the chair.

Joe tried to comfort and calm her, but she suddenly erupted, sharing the events of her afternoon. She waved her hand wildly, nearly knocking over the baby. The more she talked, the more frantic her voice became.

She just sat in the chair with little Joe, rocking and repeating, "They're closing in, but they'll never take my baby from me."

Angel's restless night of tossing and talking to herself left Joe barely able to sleep. When Joe woke up the next morning, she was gone. He could hear the rocking chair in the living room squeaking.

Joe knelt beside his bed, pouring out his sorrows to Jesus. He pleaded for his wife and son, begging for help to get the family through the fear of someone coming to take away the child.

Angel couldn't accept the idea that they had done anything wrong.

***

At work, Joe was exhausted. The only bright spot was that the cremation process took less time than usual. He expected to finish by lunchtime. However, within his first hour on the job, his supervisor called him and told him to contact the local police department.

Why would he need to contact the police? Joe's hand trembled as he slammed the gas valve shut, letting the smell of half-cooked flesh fill the building.

With his apron string still looped around his neck, elbow-length black gloves stretched over his hands and forearms, and goggles on his head, Joe sped off in his old rattletrap truck toward home, his mind racing.

Joe assumed they're closing in on Little Joe.

As his house came into sight, everything else became visible too. Blue and red lights flashed from multiple police cruisers parked along the abandoned fire tower across the street. A crowd of people gathered beneath the tower, staring up at the catwalk.

Joe dashed out of his truck and ran toward them. The crowd parted as he got closer. The police told Joe to talk to his wife and ask her not to jump. He shoved past an officer.

"Why is Angel up there?" he asked, his voice trembling with panic.

We're unsure. We parked in front of your house while walking along the sidewalk, looking for a big snake that a caller had reported. We were in front of your home when she suddenly ran out with her baby in her arms, crossed the road to the tower, and climbed up the ladder. We told her to stop because it was dangerous for the child. All she kept saying was, "You're not going to take my baby."

Joe's eyes moved closer, his gaze fixed on the officer. "Did you tell her you weren't after her baby?" Joe asked.

"Yes!" the officer ran a hand through his hair, exasperated. "But she just kept saying, 'You're not taking my baby.'"

Joe yelled at Angel, "The police officers were checking for a big snake on the loose! He took a deep breath. They did not come for little Joe!" Then he took another deep breath and said, "It's the snake you should worry about, not the police!"

Angel didn't seem to hear him at all. She started pacing back and forth on the tower catwalk, not saying a word. Her hands clenched the baby's blanket. Little Joe cried loudly.

The pastor approached Joe. "May I try speaking to Angel?" he asked, gesturing toward the tower with a hopeful look.

Please. Joe lowered his head, tears filling his eyes.

The preacher tried to comfort Angel by telling her that God loved her and the baby. Then he prayed aloud for her and the baby. For a moment, his prayer seemed to work. Angel stopped pacing and looked down at the child in her arms.

Joe pleaded with her, "Honey, please come down! No one will take the baby!"

But she yelled, "You're all in this together! You won't take my baby!" She leaned dangerously over the railing.

Angel stepped over the catwalk rails and sat on the outside of the tower's railing.

Joe dropped to his knees, crying, praying, and looking up at Angel sitting on the rails with the baby in her arms.

He begged her desperately not to jump. His voice cracked.

Joe watched as Angel slowly rose with Little Joe in her arms, leaned forward, and fell to the ground with a gut-wrenching thud.

18

Chapter 18

"HE WOULDN'T LISTEN"

Her screams echoed through Bearclaw's streets. The piercing cry caused families to wince. They knew that by dawn, Endora the witch would take someone, but who? Someone had to stop her.

Or that's what they said.

When the Piper four-seater tilted to land, Bearclaw's aerial display surprised Joel and his team. The small town of 900 residents looked like a giant clamshell on the beach; it nestled in the valley among lush green mountains and a lake. It seemed like an ideal vacation spot. All its long roads began at an intersection by the lakefront and spread outward in a fan shape, resembling a clamshell.

Despite the warm sun, he shivered. The airplane touched down on a grassy airstrip and stopped beside the waiting Bearclaw Police Department cruiser. Chief of Police Harry Wolf stood next to the cruiser and extended his hand. He grasped Joel's hand firmly; his eyes were serious. "Welcome to Bearclaw."

Joel Nabal, a paranormal investigator for the Eastern Conference of the Original Church of Jesus in Philadelphia, adjusted his tie, a nervous habit. We arrived as quickly as we could. My bishop's objections to investigating human disappearances and ghost sightings slowed us down because he was worried about my safety.

The chief nodded as he listened.

The bishop said, 'If you meddle with evil spirits, witches, and ghosts, you could tempt God.' He pointed me to Saul's consultation with the witch of Endor in the Bible.

The chief listened quietly, his expression unreadable. "After our TV network sponsors agreed to fund the trip, the bishop finally agreed. The sponsors have the right to the investigative story. So I'm glad to meet you, Chief Wolf. This is Mark, my cameraman, and Jeff, my technician." He motioned to the two men, who gave slight waves.

Chief Wolf asked, crossing his arms, "Are you sure your team can handle this job? It's a big mystery and should be told on TV."

"Yes, if your story is true, it will be," Joel said confidently with a smile.

"Jump in the cruiser, and we'll head to my office. I have coffee there, and we can talk about why we asked for your help." He paused, his gaze meeting Joel's for a moment, a flicker of genuine concern in his eyes. But... if you were me, you'd get back on that plane and go home.

A single hanging light lit the one-room police station, which didn't leave a good impression on the department. Maybe the chief's right about heading back on the plane.

But Joel stuck to his plan. "I am honored to work with an authentic Native American chief of a local tribe and chief of police." A self-satisfied expression settled on his face. Solving this mystery could catapult you and me to the big leagues. How many Native Americans have disappeared?

Uhhh ... quite a few. Chief Wolf shifted in his seat, his gaze distant. You already know about the recurring disappearances of our local tribal people and residents every two years. My father, Little Feather, was the last to disappear. He was the former tribal chief and Bearclaw's police chief. It happened two years ago, and I took his place.

Joel jotted down everything Chief Wolf said.

I have a town full of people, and not a single suspect. Several weeks ago, I found a letter slipped under my office door that said, "You're next." He slapped a weathered piece of paper onto the desk.

Hearing that, Joel's eyes widened.

To make things worse, a young college graduate spending the summer in Bearclaw wrote about the mystery of the vanishing tribal people of Bearclaw.

A national newspaper published the story, and since then, no one has visited Bearclaw. Bearclaw survives because of tourism. He shifted in his chair.

He sighed and pressed on. He pointed to the main street outside the window. The local tribe believes that a statue of Endora on Main Street comes alive whenever someone disappears. The older members of the tribe call her Jaxpe. She moves through the tribe's burial grounds.

"Be careful, Reverend Joel. The demons are said to be hungry, and traditional beliefs fade slowly." Chief Wolf's dark, serious eyes held Joel's gaze.

Here's a list of three people who have faced this horror from the start and are still in town. They're older folks. I didn't get anything from them, and I didn't give them anything in return for their help. You've got a preacher, a doctor, and a tribal medicine man.

Tell me, Chief, where's your local cemetery?

The public cemetery is west of town, while the tribal cemetery is at the foot of Bearclaw Mountain. The Tribal Council prohibits Caucasians from entering the tribal cemetery. Legend says that Endora, the witch, lives there. She collects the souls of doomed people. He leaned forward with a serious expression this time. "Do not go to the tribal cemetery."

Mark and Jeff stiffened as they exchanged glances.

You really think that, Chief?

The chief looked away, shrugged, then turned back to Joel. "The tribe forbids me from desecrating the bodies by searching through their remains for evidence. Any autopsy of a tribal member is forbidden. They would not take kindly to finding you in their sacred burial grounds. Understand, Joel?"

Joel nodded.

***

Chief Wolf arranged for Joel to interview the tribal medicine man. He isn't very eager to talk to an outsider, especially a cameraman and a technician. Joel asked the medicine man several questions about the disappearances. Joel shifted on his feet, adjusting his microphone.

He responded to questions with a simple "yes" or "no." Crossing his arms tightly over his chest. Joel sensed the medicine man's resentment of the questions.

Then the medicine man's eyes narrowed, his nose flared, his forehead creased, and he leaned toward Joel. A shadow seemed to pass over his face. "You don't believe in our tribe's religious traditions and spirits, do you?"

Not really.

"Your Holy Ghost must be mumbo jumbo, too." He paused and tapped a finger on his knee. "Tell me, Christian, of all the people missing, how many were Native Americans?"

The question stunned Joel. He swallowed hard and looked away from the medicine man's piercing eyes. "Well ... umm ... I don't know."

"I'll tell you," the medicine man seethed. He leaned in closer, his voice lowering. One! Harry's father, Little Feather. Harry Wolf's father broke tribal law by searching for the missing people in our cemetery. He took objects from the dead and refused to return them. Then he sold the objects for money.

Joel shivered. Then he asked, "What about all the other missing people?"

What others?

The other people, the one or two individuals who have disappeared every two years for the past fifty years.

Christian, how many people die each year in your area?

More than just a few each year.

That's my point. People die, but no one has disappeared here. The townspeople buried the Caucasians in the cemetery west of town and buried the Native Americans at Bearclaw Mountain. There is no mystery about that.

Joel furrowed his brow, uncertain.

"The mystery in Bearclaw is why people live so long." He paused. "That's what you should investigate." With no response from Joel, he continued. "The ghost of Jaxpe came and ate Little Feather as punishment for violating tribal law."

The two men exchanged glances.

"Jaxpe feeds on the sins and shame of our people. You are not Native American. But you be careful. Demons are hungry for flesh." The medicine man let out a faint smile.

This was the second time someone warned Joel about the hungry demons, and he felt confused.

The medicine man stood up and quietly left the interview.

***

The retired doctor from Bearclaw arrived unexpectedly at the police station. A male nurse helped the old gentleman inside. The doctor wheezed, coughed, and struggled to walk, let alone sit in a wooden folding chair. He apologized for his disability.

After the crew set up the camera, Joel asked, "Do you have any evidence or theories about the legend of people disappearing?"

"No," said the doctor. He clenched the wooden armrest tightly. "I don't believe in the hocus-pocus paranormal. All the people who disappeared were old, except for Little Feather. And people say he died twenty years ago."

"Twenty years?" Joel narrowed his eyes.

That's a pretty lengthy explanation. When people claim these individuals disappeared, they craft a convincing story. Because deaths happen every two years, the story seems suspicious yet convincing.

Joel wondered why Chief Harry said his father, Little Feather, had died just two years ago. If the doctor is right, why would Harry lie?

"I'm eighty-three." He chuckled dryly. "I'm considered young. I've never figured out how people here live so long. I convinced myself it's the fresh air in the mountains."

How old is Chief Harry?

He is 84 years old.

Joel shook his head in disbelief.

Our local tribe believes Jaxpe ate the missing people, which is absurd. In my research, medical history shows that uneducated people, folk religion, and survival situations often lead to cannibalism. Cannibalism seems like a more believable explanation.

Thanks, doctor. You've given helpful information. Could you tell me where the preacher lives?

He lives on Front Street, the same street where the statue of Endora stands. It's an icon locals and visitors alike talk about. People have told them it's a statue of Jaxpe, the man-eater. Please stop by the preacher's house and ask his nanny to make you some tea. They say it will make you feel young. I'm skeptical, but some say the tea can even extend your life.

***

Walking down Main Street with Mark and Jeff, Joel saw the local barber sitting on a bench outside his shop, reading a newspaper. Joel sat on the barber's bench to chat with him.

The barber asked, "What is a famous ghost chaser like you doing walking downtown? I thought you would be riding in a limousine."

I'm on my way to see the preacher, but I saw you and figured I'd ask a question.

Shoot, ghost man.

Who made the statue of the witch Endora?

The barber laughed so hard he nearly lost his breath.

Have you seen the statue, mister?

"No."

The preacher's mother placed it there. She had it made to honor him when he graduated from the Native American Divinity College. He is half Native American. The Latin word "Praedicator" is inscribed at the bottom, meaning "preacher." Locals are unaware of its meaning. He lets them believe it is Endora or Jaxpe. It depends on who he's speaking with—the local natives or the tourists.

Joel said, "I assume you don't believe in the paranormal."

I can't even spell the word. Someone tricked you into believing a fairy tale. They made the statue out of stone based on a picture of the preacher's graduation attire. They wore Indian robes with long, wavy wigs. The preacher embellishes stories of Endora or Jaxpe to attract tourists.

Joel tilted his head in surprise.

The college kid wrote a fictional story about people disappearing to sell books and attract tourists to Bearclaw. But instead of drawing visitors, panic spread, and people started leaving," the barber shook his head.

Bearclaw's Board of Aldermen believed that a famous ghost hunter like you could put Bearclaw on TV and draw tourists back to town. Harry supported the 'disappearing people' story to attract tourists. He tells people that townsfolk die every two years, just like clockwork, including his father. It's all a façade.

Joel now shook his head along with the barber.

Visit the preacher's house and ask him to show you his graduation photo. You'll notice he looks similar to the statue. If you want more details, talk to the nanny; she lives with him. She's 105 years old. Be sure to try her tea—it's the best in town. Something about it makes you feel young again.

Joel thanked the barber for the information, even though he felt a bit foolish. Then he headed to the preacher's house.

***

Joel knocked on the preacher's door, but no one answered. He was about to leave when a white-haired, hunched-shouldered woman dressed in a long white gown stepped out from the side of the house. Based on the symbols on her dress and her skin tone, Joel guessed that the local tribe possibly employed her as a nanny.

"May I help you?" she asked.

I'm trying to locate the preacher.

He isn't here, and I don't know when he'll return.

Joel introduced himself as a Christian minister and told her that, along with Mark and Jeff, he was investigating the legend of the Bearclaw people who had disappeared. "People know me as a paranormal investigator."

The lady looked at Joel and smiled. Please come into the house and honor our home by having some refreshments. I can answer your questions. I have been the preacher's nanny since he was born. Please come in.

The three followed her into the living room, where she prepared and served tea, and Mark set up the camera. As they sipped their tea, Joel's questions kept coming.

"How old are you?" he asked.

One hundred five.

How old is the preacher?

"Ninety."

How can you be 105? You don't look even close to that.

The preacher has a special food and drink that makes you look younger, and I feel sixty. He doesn't reveal his ingredients. You can taste a hint of meat flavor in the tea.

"Yes," this tea is delicious. I believe I detect a hint of liver flavor.

The nanny smiled.

Is the preacher partly Native American from the local tribe?

Yes, his father was the chief religious leader of our tribe. His mother was the daughter of a miner who was digging for gold in our mountains. I am his half-sister. The preacher is our current chief religious leader. He is preparing for the great dance that he will soon lead.

"Where is the preacher now?" Joel asked.

He is at the Indian graveyard preparing for the dance. He is fasting and praying for all his people, living and dead. You may find him in his prep room at the cemetery. She took a deep breath. "Preacher Nabal, do you believe in the afterlife?"

Yes, but not in the same way as ghost and witch stories.

She nodded. "Do you believe people can transfer power through flesh consumption?"

"No."

The preacher says Jesus did.

"That is absurd," Joel said, shaking his head. What about the law that a Caucasian may not go into the Indian cemetery?

"That is a local legend. No such law exists," the nanny laughed.

What about Endora, the witch? Is she for real? She laughed again.

There's nothing to worry about. Someone is using her image and her screams as a prank on the locals. Do you know how to get to the cemetery?

No, I'm sorry.

I'll ask our gardener, Tom, to help you.

"But it's getting dark. We won't be able to see," Joel said. He didn't like graveyards at night.

She chuckled. "Tom is a Native American."

After leaving the preacher's house, Mark and Jeff told Joel they weren't going into a Native American graveyard at night. "People warned us". If you do, you're on your own. People have told you twice about being eaten by demons and breaking the laws of the natives' graveyard, and you're ignoring the warnings. Whether they're true or not, aren't you even a little scared?"

"No, not at all. I'm an investigator. I don't buy into tourist tales." Joel blushed.

Don't you believe that God doesn't want you to tempt him? asked Jeff.

"What has God got to do with this?" I am not tempting him. I have a job to do. If I break a few rules, who cares? God hasn't the time to waste on such frivolous concerns."

***

Joel followed Tom to the center of the Indian cemetery, where someone had set up a tent. At the tent's entrance, a large white sheet hung. Someone had attached a portable cassette tape player and pinned it to a wire running up the mountain. Joel wondered if they used to send messages to the village below.

A voice inside the tent spoke in Indian, a language Joel did not understand. Then the voice said, "Please come in."

The preacher sat at a round table with three others. Wearing traditional Indian clothing, he invited Tom and Joel to join him for a celebratory meal. The preacher served stewed liver with potatoes, bread, and the special brew tea.

"How did you know we were coming?" Joel asked.

I am beyond mortal. I can't explain it; you wouldn't understand. My friend Endora saw you coming.

The preacher asked Joel to give thanks for the meal, and they ate. After eating the stewed liver, Joel sat in his chair, sipping the same tea the nanny once served him, but this cup of tea tasted even better than the nanny's.

Joel said, "This is the best meal of liver, bread, and tea I have ever eaten."

Joel Nabal said his final words.

***

Joel's bishop, the doctor, and a TV network executive stood inside the hospital morgue over the black body bag.

The doctor said, "This is the strangest case I have ever seen. There isn't any explanation. The autopsy revealed that someone had removed the liver, but there are no incisions or scars."

"I never imagined that something like this could happen," the TV executive said.

The bishop grimaced. "After his death, the town of Bearclaw awarded Joel a strange medal of honor."

"For what?" the doctor asked.

"For the Man Who Wouldn't Listen."

The other two men looked confused.

The bishop took a deep breath. Someone had attached a note to Joel's body: 'You shall not tempt the Lord thy God.'

19

Chapter 19

"EBER"

Eber came from a proud family of servants in King David's household. The time had come for Eber to serve King Solomon as the chief engineer for waste management. But today, things would change.

Young, ambitious, and trained, Eber, along with two chambermaids, entered the bedchamber of one of King Solomon's wives—Princess Zarephath. The maids immediately began to change the bed linens, replace the old flowers with new ones, and scrub the floor, all in anticipation of the princess's return from breakfast.

Unexpectedly, she returned early. "Don't mind me. Keep working. I must get ready to host a royal guest." She sat in front of the polished metal mirror by her bed, combing her long auburn hair.

Eber approached her. "May I replace the chamber pot under your bed with a fresh one, Princess?" She dismissively waved her hand.

Yes, and hurry up! I need to change my clothes.

He crouched behind the princess's chair and reached beneath the bed for the chamber pot. The old baked clay pot was heavy and took up a lot of space. He pulled it gently by one of the handles when the lid slipped off and clanged under the bed. The contents could easily slosh out if the pot jostled.

After the pot cleared the bed, Eber picked it up by its handles. But one of the handles broke.

The pot tipped over.

He tried to grab it with the broken piece still in his hand.

But urine and feces splashed out.

All over Princess Zarephath's long hair and neck, it spilled out. The pee and poop soaked her blouse with nasty, disgusting filth.

Everything spiraled into hysteria.

The princess shouted for the guards. She sobbed and cursed at Eber in a wild fury. "Put him in the dungeon! Chop off his head!"

Eber, standing five feet four inches tall with a round waist, long hair covering his ears, rosy cheeks, and a red nose, said nothing. The guards led him away to the dungeon with the chamber pot still in his hand.

***

Tamar watched from her window for her husband's return. The food grew cold, a signal that something was wrong. Darkness almost swallowed the shadows of the trees. Eber rarely came home this late.

Tamr's questions piled up in her mind. Where is Eber? What has happened? Should I find him? Someone knocked on her door.

She peered through a hole in the white cloth hanging over the small window in the door. A soldier from King Solomon's army stood at the door. She feared the worst had happened to her husband.

"Yes?" she said through the door. "Can I help you?"

I have information about Eber.

Tamar opened the door and greeted the soldier as he entered.

Please tell me.

The soldier explained that her husband had insulted Princess Zarephath, one of King Solomon's wives, when he spilled a chamber pot on her. She ordered him to the dungeon to await punishment from King Solomon.

Can I go to the dungeon and see him?

No. King Solomon will judge later.

***

Eber sat in the darkness of the dungeon, with his arms chained above his head, exhausted, embarrassed, and hungry. He begged the guards for just one thing: to look after his wife and comfort her with someone by her side. At first, the guards dismissed him. But he kept pleading until one guard finally grumbled that he would take care of it.

A voice from the dark dungeon asked, "What are you in for, mister?"

"Leave me alone."

Come, my good man. I am in chains just like you, right around the corner. No one else here wants to talk anymore. With little food or water given to me, chained and sitting in my urine and feces, a little friendly conversation would really help me. Please talk to me.

"What do you want to know?" Eber asked, biting his lip.

What are you in here for?

I worked as King Solomon's top sanitation engineer.

We entered the bedchamber of one of King Solomon's wives. I pulled the chamber pot from under the bed and tried to exchange it. The handle broke, the pot tilted in my hand, and the feces and urine spilled over Princess Zarephath.

The stranger started to chuckle, then grew into a full-blown laugh. His contagious laughter made Eber laugh. Soon, the entire prison dungeon echoed with loud laughter, prompting the guards to come in and quiet everyone down. You could hear the prisoners' chains jingle with their laughter.

Job, the other prisoner, lamented the past foolishness that got him in trouble and, worse, left his family destitute.

Eber couldn't sleep at all that night. Worrying about his wife and the dungeon's snoring concert kept sleep away from him. Frightened and barely able to see the predawn light in the darkness of the dungeon, Eber cringed when the men with torches came for him the next morning.

One of the men, holding a long chain of keys, introduced himself as the dungeon superintendent. The superintendent then introduced the other man as King Solomon.

Eber attempted to sit up properly, but the chains kept him from looking respectable.

Your Majesty, I apologize for my disrespect and my confinement. I earnestly ask you to consider my intentions in Princess Zarephath's bedchamber. I didn't spill the chamber pot's contents onto Princess Zarephath on purpose. The devil broke the handle of the chamber pot. I beg for my life, but more than that, I suffer knowing the shame I have brought upon my wife. Please have mercy on her.

"Superintendent," the King said, "unchain this honorable man."

The superintendent unlocked and removed the shackles. Eber sighed with relief and softly rubbed his wrists.

When this happened, instead of focusing on yourself, you thought about the burden you placed on your wife. One of the guards told me you wouldn't stop asking them to take care of her. Because of that, I consider you a wise and honorable man.

The King paused and then continued. "Then, at night, the palace guard woke me because of a distressed woman at the palace door. At first, I dismissed her urgent plea to appear before me at such a late hour. But as I lay in bed, she kept wailing and pleading her case for an audience with me. It echoed not only through the palace halls but also into the city streets. And I realized she was your wife."

He stared deeply into Eber's eyes. "The Lord God spoke to me in my heart through His Spirit and said, 'What if it were your wife wailing and pleading in the night for help?'"

He paused, as if reliving the experience. "At midnight, I granted her request for an audience with me. I listened to her plea, and I thought of your concern for her. Despite my many wives, I never knew the quality of your marriage or the love and care you shared with your wife. Last night, your wife redeemed you."

Solomon pursed his lips and looked down. "I summoned Zarephath to appear before me. After hearing the plea as I did, Zarephath regretted demanding your life."

Eber sighed and then smiled.

But protocol requires me to enforce some form of punishment to maintain Zarephath's dignity and decorum in the king's household.

Eber ceased smiling.

Your punishment is: You are now the headmaster of the dunghill. You will be in charge of this place, from which most men run away, and you will employ servants to assist you. Your task is to find a better purpose for the dunghill than being a disgusting waste and a foul nuisance. After a year, you will come before me for assessment.

Thank you, King Solomon.

"And thank you, Eber, for your noble character."

May I hire a servant from this dungeon? I fear no one else will accept my task.

Who would that be?

Your servant Job is nearby. His foolish mistake also led to his imprisonment. However, he is still an honorable man.

I remember him. King Solomon paused thoughtfully. "Very well." He assigned Job to the dunghill under Eber's supervision for a one-year evaluation. Then King Solomon left the dungeon. In the desert heat, Eber and Job sat near the huge dunghill. The smell made it hard to breathe, and the constant buzzing of camel flies drove them crazy.

Well, Eber, do you have any ideas on what to do with this pile of feces and urine?

No. Our King spared our lives only to mock us with the idea of freedom, using it to tackle an impossible problem. We might lose both.

Job began praying to God for help. But Eber's thoughts stayed on Tamar—her stubborn boldness in front of the King and how she would continue to suffer because of this mess.

***

After a guard told her about the men's conditional release, Tamar prepared lunch for them and found them sitting near the foul-smelling dunghill. Job swatted away the camel flies, while Eber stared into the desert sand. The two men showed a duet of hopelessness.

When Eber saw her, he jumped to his feet and hugged her tightly, kissing her passionately, so much so that Job looked away in embarrassment.

"My husband," she said, "why do you sit here loathing the dunghill? Do you have a solution for using it? After learning about your plight from a friendly guard, I told him you would have no problem because you are the wisest man in the world. You would find a useful purpose for the dunghill."

I have let you down, my love. He shrugged. "I am sorry."

Please don't despair, my husband. We will discuss it after lunch. Let's eat under that Joshua tree, upwind from the stench of the dunghill.

Job burped from his lunch while listening to alternating despairs and encouragements from Eber and Tamar. Then they sat silently under the Joshua tree.

Tamar got up and gathered their scraps. "There should be a different way to use scraps instead of tossing them onto the desert sand. All that does is encourage the grass to grow faster."

Eber sat up straight.

Garbage? Growth?

He remembered a proverb that people often repeated in the palace. Something like, "A wife of noble character who can find, and her husband trusts in her, and he will have no lack of good things."

He leaned forward and looked at Tamar so closely that it frightened her.

What's wrong?

You are an angel from God with the answer to our problem.

"What answer?" Job asked.

If you leave the fish scraps there, they will stink. However, when planted, they help the grass grow—that which stinks helps plants grow. Job's eyes widened, and his mouth spread into a smile.

Tamar grabbed Eber's arm in shock of realization.

Then Job finally understood. "Great Abraham! Eber, you're brilliant!"

Job, a skilled metalsmith, dug a pit in the ground and built an iron grid cover to sift ashes from burning waste and leftover animal scraps.

He crushed rocks to grind bones into powder, then spread the powder over dried feces. He enlisted friends to level a flat area where they could mix all the ingredients and spread them across the fields and gardens.

Eber supervised as the workers spread the feces to dry and helped Tamar collect containers to carry them into the fields and gardens. Many workers had to spread the mysterious substance by hand across the farmland and home gardens, washing their hands frequently. Handwashing. If successful, this grueling, foul-smelling job would bring great prosperity to the people and King Solomon.

Tamar would gather the first fruits of the harvest from farmers and neighbors to pay the King and support the royal family's needs. However, this plan relied on faith in God. They had to wait and pray for a successful growing season. Time would show the results.

***

When the growing season began, clouds gathered, and rain fell. Days after the rain, seeds sprouted and pushed their shoots toward the warm sunshine. Hope and excitement filled everyone's hearts.

Seeing the green fields eased Job and Eber's worries about King Solomon's upcoming judgment. Still, they had to wait for the harvest. Fortunately, the long growing season ended without any natural disasters.

The fields produced large crops in the first harvest season. Every day, they carried heavy loads to the market and the King's palace.

King Solomon gathered the people for a public service to give thanks to God for the increase.

After giving thanks to God, King Solomon ordered Eber, Tamar, and Job to stand before the assembly and face judgment for their one-year assessment. The King stood silently before the assembly, showing no expression on his face.

Then he said, "With God, nothing is impossible. Today, we see those words fulfilled through the blessings of our harvest. God used his servants Eber, Tamar, and Job to bring Him glory. Yet I must deliver judgment upon them as originally decreed."

When Eber saw the King's expression, he lost hope of gaining his freedom. Tamar began to cry, and Job lifted his hands to heaven, praising the Lord for the joy of serving him.

King Solomon loudly declared, "According to their deeds, I appoint Eber, Tamar, and Job, the servants of God, as Ministers of Agriculture for the entire kingdom. Therefore, from this day forward, they and their families will live in the king's palace and dine at his table."

Eber remembered a psalm that people said King David, Solomon's father, had written, and he believed it. It went something like, 'A righteous man may face many troubles, but the Lord carries him through each one.'

20

Chapter 20

"YOUR REFLECTION"

Bart sat on his bed, gazing at his reflection in the mirror on the bedroom door, talking to himself while contemplating his last chance to attend prom. It's been four years, and I still haven't gone to a prom.

After four years of high school, Bart never went to prom because he didn't have a girlfriend. The only time a girl even considered being friends with him was in fifth grade, when Nancy Williams passed a note asking him to be her boyfriend.

Before he could return the note, the teacher caught it. When the teacher asked who had given him the note, Bart refused to say anything. He's no snitch. The teacher didn't like him anyway. Even after she paddled him in front of his classmates, Bart wouldn't tell on Nancy. That was the closest he ever came to having a girlfriend.

By high school, other students would giggle as he walked past. They would say things like, "There goes the ugliest person who has ever lived. A total loser." From what Bart saw in the mirror, they were right. He traced the outline of his reflection with his finger, a bitter taste in his mouth.

To make things worse, Bart was so unattractive that during PE classes, no one wanted to pick him for their team. People considered a team unlucky if they chose the last person remaining. They always left him for later.

How could my miserable life possibly get worse?

Feeling overwhelmed and exhausted, he considered a way to escape this world. A bead of sweat traced a cold line down his temple.

But his conscience questioned: "Is this what Jesus would do?" He swallowed the lump in his throat, and his hand trembled. Anger and frustration drove Bart to stand in front of the full-length mirror on the door and examine himself.

He looked at his reflection. "Mirror, mirror on the door, who is the ugliest person of all?"

He half expected the mirror to reply.

"Okay, I'm too ugly for you to answer." He stood there in a daze. Then, for no particular reason other than to distract himself from his pain, he said, "Try this, magic mirror." Broken, you're useless too. What will happen then?

He lifted his leg and kicked his shoe against the mirror.

Swoosh—crash—splat!

***

Bart sat in front of a beige camping tent in a hot desert, spitting out hot sand and dirt while he sat on the ground.

What happened?

He remembered his mother's warning: "Broken mirrors bring bad things."

Did he walk through the mirror? Where was he? He couldn't believe what he saw: a vast desert of sand with tents of various shapes and colors arranged in tidy rows.

A woman stepped out of the tent and looked at him. "Bartholomew, did you spill the water bucket again? Go back to the well and get another bucket of water." She nodded toward the end of the row of tents. "Hurry, the family's ready to eat supper."

Bartholomew? Bart was confused, but he decided he should get a bucket of water for this lady. He looked in the direction she had nodded and saw an old, round stone well with a grass-covered roof and a rope-and-crank bucket. Nearby, a girl about his age with curly black hair was there, lifting a bucket of water.

He stood and noticed he was wearing a long tunic instead of a shirt and pants, with sandals instead of penny loafers.

Where am I?

He went up to the girl at the well and asked, "Hello. Are you getting water?"

The girl looked at him with a curious squint. "What do you think I'm getting from a well?" she asked before turning away and walking off.

Wait! What's your name? What do you call this place?

"Bartholomew, stop this. You know my name is Samara. We live in Abel-Meholah, Israel. We're in eighth grade. I live three tents down from you."

"Wait, Samara, and I will carry your water bucket along with mine."

Why would the most handsome boy in our town want to carry my water bucket?

Because the most beautiful girl in town shouldn't have to carry a water bucket.

She cast a shy glance at Bartholomew and said, "Maybe I'll wait."

Bartholomew hurried to grab the bucket of water. He couldn't believe what was happening. After everything, he didn't care what world he was in. He kept thinking, "Thank you, Lord!" as they walked away, smiling at each other. Now, a girl—a beautiful girl—thought he was handsome.

That night, the supper his supposed family ate together was awkward. He watched his supposed mother and family eat roasted lamb and vegetable soup on a lamb's ear, or he hoped. The bread was hard and tasteless. He kept looking for a saltshaker but never found one. He didn't ask.

Their conversation was also confusing. His apparent father read the biblical Passover story from a scroll. He knew the story, but didn't grasp that God had sent the death angel. Why would God kill people?

Nevertheless, later that night, Bartholomew fell asleep on a small pallet on the floor.

***

In the early morning hours, his supposed father woke him up. "Wake up, Bartholomew! They're here!"

Who, what... what are you talking about?

The infidel Naaman, the Syrian general, attacked our camp.

Bartholomew's father stood at the entrance of their tent with his sickle, ready to defend his family. Several of the guards watching the camp had died in the early morning raid by the invaders. However, a swift response from the soldiers on duty repelled the attack, though the raiders carried off several people.

Bartholomew's apparent father told him to meet at sunrise to assess the damage. During the meeting, they learned that raiders had burned their barley fields.

The raiders also scattered their flocks and herds of sheep, goats, and cattle across the countryside. After assessing the damage to their livestock—including what wolves, other people, and the invaders had taken during the raid—the herders estimated that about two-thirds of their animals had been taken by raiders and predators.

The painful list of missing people included Samara. Several community leaders questioned prisoners captured during the attack and gathered information on where the invaders took their people.

The community's priest advised the men to go home, prepare for war, and volunteer for strike forces to rescue their people.

Bartholomew's father heated his forge to soften his plowshare. When it was hot enough, he hammered his plowshare into a sword and a spearhead. As he finished shaping his sword and spear, several men passed by, and Bart overheard their plans.

During the raid, Naaman's soldiers took three women and two children. Naaman's wife wanted to bring more female servants. She lived separately from her husband because he was a leper. Bartholomew's community had just learned about Naaman's leprosy.

He asked his father where Naaman's wife lived. His father described the home of Naaman's first wife in Damascus. She was older than his other wives. She had no children and needed new servants. She preferred child servants.

Why are you interested in that information?

Bartholomew said, "I want to rescue Samara, my new friend. I hope to make her eventually my wife."

Son, you have to go through a desert full of wild animals and bandits. You need to carry all your water and food with you. You're still young and small. I don't know.

"I can do this, Father!"

"Sounds like you got the love bug, Bartholomew. You dream big for a kid. How do you plan to rescue her?"

I will pray to the Son of God, Jesus. He will guide me.

Who is this... Jesus, you're talking about?

"He is the Son of God, and God sent him from heaven to earth to die for the sins of humankind. You don't know him yet, and I have things to tell you, but I don't have time to explain them now. You must give me your permission to leave now to rescue Samara."

Son, I don't understand Jesus, but you have my permission to leave—though I don't have an extra weapon to give you for your quest. Don't you think it would be safer to try a rescue with a group rather than alone? You're too inexperienced to do this.

No, Father. I believe Jesus sent me to you here and now for this purpose. On my own, I can travel faster than a group and blend in with the Aramean people. If no one notices me, I can locate the hostages better than a group of raiders forcing their way into a city. Jesus will take care of me.

"Jesus, Jesus. I need to learn about this Jesus," his father said. "For now, take my ring and go to our guard station at the yellow-striped tent at the edge of our village. Ask for Captain Joel. Tell him your story. With this ring, you have my permission to rescue Samara. He will explain the enemy's whereabouts and give you instructions on how to reach them. You will be our spy. "God be with you, son."

***

After Captain Joel gave him permission and directions, Bartholomew started walking north toward the Aramean city of Damascus. He could have ridden a camel, which would have been faster yet more conspicuous.

After three long days of walking, Bart arrived in the early morning hours, still dark. With limited visibility, he crept through the streets, scouting for lookouts and guards. One small campfire flickered near a well. A guard must have been tending the fire. He had learned that night guards often sat by wells.

Bartholomew was tired and hungry. His adoptive mother had packed several corn dodgers and fig cakes for his journey. He found a low mound of sand that someone had shoveled from the community's privy. He settled behind the sand pile made from the dirt and ate the last corn dodger, then fell asleep.

He woke up in the afternoon after most people had replenished their water for the day. But two women came to the well to draw water in the cool of early evening. His heart nearly stopped. One of them was Samara.

Bartholomew pulled his keffiyeh over his head and covered his face with his veil. He approached the women at the well and greeted them. They nodded, lifted their jugs, and prepared to leave. Bartholomew followed closely.

"Samara," he whispered.

She paused and looked at him, her eyes wide.

Are you ready to go before we leave this place?

Show your face, stranger.

Bartholomew lowered his veil.

Shock hit Samara, and she couldn't respond. The other woman paused and looked back.

After she regains her composure, Samara turns away from him. "Ignore me. They are watching me."

They all started walking again.

Just out of the other woman's hearing, Samara whispered, "Follow me at a distance to Naaman's wife's estate just ahead. At midnight, meet me in the garden behind the house."

***

At midnight, Samara arrived. Bartholomew waited anxiously for her.

He grabbed her shoulders. "Come with me. We can be far from here before they find out you're missing."

I don't think that's wise, Bartholomew.

Why?

Since we will be walking and running, they will ride horses and track us with dogs. There must be another way. They'll recapture me, and they'll enslave you.

His heart dropped like a stone into the ocean.

So they sat quietly on a garden bench, holding each other. She snuggled into Bartholomew's arms until dawn.

Bartholomew quietly prayed to God, pleading for guidance on how to escape safely with Samara. She listened to his prayer and hugged him tightly until he finished.

Bartholomew said, "I have an answer from God. The strangest thing about it is that I already knew about it."

She looked at him. "What?"

Tell Naaman's wife that Naaman should go to Israel and see the prophet, Elisha. He can heal Naaman's leprosy. Elisha, God's prophet, has healed lepers before. But Naaman must agree to free everyone his raiders captured from our village when he returns.

How do you know? How can you say all of this?

Well, I saw it somewhere.

Bartholomew trusted God's Holy Word more than ever.

***

A few hours later, while doing her morning chores, Samara told Naaman's wife about God's prophet in Israel. Elisha could heal people from leprosy. Naaman's wife shared the news with Naaman.

Without saying goodbye, Naaman took Samara, a servant girl, with his entourage to Israel to meet Elisha the prophet.

***

When Bartholomew learned from Naaman's servants that Samara had gone with Naaman to Israel, he felt distressed and overwhelmed. He fasted and prayed for Naaman's healing and for Samara's safe return.

The next day, Bartholomew began working as a gardener in Naaman's household. Each day was another struggle as he waited for Samara's safe return. Finally, on the seventh day, they returned. Naaman gathered the people at the public well.

Standing before the crowd, Bartholomew cringed in fear when he saw

Naaman's guards, prompting Samara to step forward and face the people. It looked like a public shaming of a criminal about to be executed by the authorities.

Samara looked scared and nervous. Naaman had promised that if the prophet Elisha healed him, he would release her and the hostages his men had taken from her village. But no one knew if he would keep his word.

Naaman rode a black Arabian horse as he approached the people of Damascus. His cloak and keffiyeh obscured his face and body. No one could tell if Naaman was healed.

Naaman dismounted his horse and motioned for the crowd to listen. "Today I declare the God of Israel the one true God." I am a worshipper of the god Rimmon, whom I sought many times to heal my leprosy, but he could not heal me.

This girl, from Israel, told me about the prophet Elisha, the healer of lepers. Doubting her word and fearing the death penalty for lying, I took her with me to meet Prophet Elisha.

At first, he insulted me by telling me to wash in the muddy Jordan River. I declined his request. But after my son counseled me, I agreed to bathe in the muddy river. Instantly, I was healed by the only God of Israel. I hereby declare his name today.

Naaman took off his keffiyeh and cloak to show that he had been healed of leprosy. The crowd gasped and then cheered.

If this young lady hadn't told my wife about God's prophet, Elisha, I wouldn't have received healing. By my agreement with her, I officially declare that all Israelites my men captured are free.

Naaman arranged transportation and protection for the captives' return to Israel. Bartholomew followed all the way at a distance.

Passing strangers told Samara's village about the miracle of Naaman and his proclamation of freedom for all captured Israelites.

When they returned to their home village, the people greeted them with a grand celebration. Bartholomew's adoptive parents and Samara's parents were the first to welcome them.

Samara's parents invited Bartholomew and his adoptive parents to dine with them at their tent. When Bartholomew entered, everything went dark—and then there was nothing.

***

Mysteriously, Bart suddenly appeared sitting on his bed, staring at his reflection in the door mirror. He couldn't believe he had returned home and lost the only girl he'd ever loved—and who had ever loved him.

"Oh, God, why have you forsaken me? Why did you bring me back? There is nothing here for me but death." Bart stepped up to the magic mirror and tried to push his hand through it. The mirror no longer worked its magic. He tried several more times to put his hand through the mirror, but only banged it against the glass.

What he went through couldn't have just been a dream. It was real.

He threw himself onto his bed, looked up to heaven with tears in his eyes, and prayed. "You said that if I could believe, then a believer can do all things. Is it true, or is it a lie?"

No response.

Silence filled the room.

Then there was a knock at his bedroom door. His mother's voice said, "Bart, you have a phone call from a girl."

A girl?

Startled, he asked, "What is her name?"

"Samara."

About the Author

Brother Grady A. Simpson is an American Christian Fiction Author. With degrees in Public School Administration, Law Enforcement Technology, and Pastoral Ordination, he uses his experiences to create clean, faith-based stories of mystery, suspense, and crime.

He lives in eastern North Carolina with his wife, children, and wonderful grandchildren. Want to see more? Visit brothergasbooks.com.

You can connect with me on:

- https://www.brothergasbooks.com
- https://www.facebook.com/profile.php?id=61577028030315&sk=about

www.ingramcontent.com/pod-product-compliance
Lightning Source LLC
LaVergne TN
LVHW010700110826
845149LV00014B/3179

* 9 7 9 8 9 9 4 8 2 0 8 0 3 *